Blue Spirit
A Tipsy Fairy Tale

E. Chris Garrison

Cover art: Anne Rosario

Editor: Scott M. Sandridge

Copy Editor: Amy E. Garrison

Published by Silly Hat Books

ISBN: 978-1-953763-20-4

www.sillyhatbooks.com

Publisher's Note:

Blue Spirit is a work of fiction. All names, characters, and places are the product of the author's imagination, used in fictitious manner. Any resemblances to actual persons, places, locales, events, etc. are purely coincidental.

Printed in the United States of America

Third Edition

Other books by E. Chris Garrison

Reality Check: A Tale of Quantum Entanglements
Alien Beer and Other Stories

Trans-Continental: Girl in the Gears
Trans-Continental: Mississippi Queen

Blue Spirit: A Tipsy Fairy Tale
Restless Spirit: A Tipsy Fairy Tale
Mean Spirit: A Tipsy Fairy Tale

The Road Ghosts Omnibus

Contains:
Book One: Four 'til Late
Book Two: Sinking Down
Book Three: Me and the Devil
Short Story: Spectral Delivery

Dedication and Acknowledgements

Blue Spirit is dedicated to my friends and family.
Thank you for cheering me on and believing in me.

This book would not have been written
without the support of these people:
Amy, Heather, Heather, Pam, Karin, Sara,
Billy, Judith, Kathy, Becky, Lisa, Amanda,
Joe, Craig, Kerra, Karl and Mom

Chapter One

I could tell by the way my shadow jumped up and down that Minnie wanted my attention. She picked an inconvenient time for it too, rolling down the road on a bus, on my way to work the afternoon shift at Starbucks. In order to talk to her, even see her, I'd have to take a swig of vodka from the flask I keep in my roomy purse.

I looked around at my fellow passengers. A matron in teddy bear scrubs warmed the whole left side of my body as we sat facing the aisle. I could imagine her sweat mingling with mine in the summer heat. On my right, a little teenage skater boy kept sneaking looks up at me. I didn't care for the creepy way he kept scrunching up closer every time I caught him looking. But he seemed harmless, so I decided he could have the cheap thrill as long as he continued to mind his manners before one of us reached our respective stop.

My shadow waved at me, frantic about getting my attention. I sighed and rolled my eyes. Minnie could be quite insistent. *Fine, I'll risk it this once.*

The crammed bus bumped along, every seat filled. Some people stood, hanging onto rails. A stop was requested.

We three swayed together, right then left, as the bus slowed and stopped. I took the opportunity to pretend to drop my purse. The bus hissed and groaned as it "kneeled" to be closer to the ground for the departing and boarding passengers. I leaned over and set my fast food drink cup on the floor and popped the top. I felt sneaky and a little guilty as I slipped my flask out of my purse and tipped it into the open cup. The leftover ice crackled and popped as the alcohol flowed over it. I sealed the lid and screwed my flask shut and hoped no one saw me put it back.

I heard the doors slap shut, and someone's feet almost stepped on my purse, so I sat up and stared ahead of me without looking at anyone. I crossed my feet at the ankles, the chains on my boots tinkling against each other. The nurse matron was sitting stiffer next to me on one side, and I felt the stare of the skater boy on the other heating up the side of my face. Damn, they noticed. Oh well, nothing to lose now. I sipped at the alcohol and watery flat diet coke and felt the familiar warmth spread down and throughout my body. I took a deep breath and enjoyed the sensation, pretending for a moment that I didn't care what the strangers pressing me on either side thought.

I opened my eyes and looked down where my shadow had been jerking and jumping around. It was back to being just my shadow but leaning on the toe of my left boot was Minnie. Short for mini-me, since the resemblance is uncanny. Except she's a little scrunched and squat, where I'm tall and "willowy" as everyone says. She's also got little vampire fangs and jet-black hair, where mine's just plain dishwater blonde. Today she wore a gauzy navy blue cloud of a dress she could have stolen from a plus-sized Barbie doll.

Minnie grinned up at me and blew me a kiss. Conscious of my neighbors once again, I wrinkled my nose in irritation at the fairy. Well, okay, so she's not a fairy, and neither are the other beings I see when I've had a little bit to drink. Then again, I suspect they're what inspired fairy stories in the first place. The creatures just hate the name. I think that's because these days, most people think of pretty little things like Tinker Bell, rather than the scarier beings in the Brothers Grimm stories.

Minnie stuck her tongue out at me and favored me with a syrupy smile, "I'll bet you didn't notice. Again. You really should pay better attention, Skye!"

No one could hear her but me, but I couldn't answer out loud. Not unless I wanted people to think I was crazy, talking to myself. I mean, the bus *is* the place to do that sort of thing, if you're so inclined. I see some of these people on a regular basis, so they don't need to think that kind of thing about me. Sure, maybe I am a little crazy. Plenty of my friends and acquaintances think so. It's nothing serious in any case, and many people think my eccentricities are endearing. What can I say? I'm just charming that way. Humble, too.

I pursed my lips and furrowed my brow, imagining that I looked stern. Minnie laughed and pointed. For a moment, I thought she was pointing at me, but I followed her finger to the skater boy next to me. It was my turn to sneak a glance.

The kid looked away, down at his feet. His shoes were two different color Converse canvas shoes, one red and one black, both weathered to the point of fraying around the edges. His socks didn't match either, one was striped green and black, the other striped orange and blue. He wore dirty khaki shorts big enough to accommodate two of him, cinched around his hips with a belt. His blue moon-and-stars boxers rose a couple of inches above the waistband of his shorts. His bright green Incredible Hulk t-shirt looked newer than his other clothes. A furry hat held down his shaggy hair. Except that's not all I saw. You know those pictures they sell around Halloween time? The ones where you think you see a dignified man in a Victorian suit, but when you move to the right a little, the picture changes to show him with rotting zombie flesh, exposed bones? Well, that's how I see some people when alcohol allows me to see with my second sight.

The other image I saw of this kid was of a wolf-man, the hat revealed to be real furry ears, his wolfish grin literal now, complete with tongue lolling over sharp teeth.

He caught me looking and grinned even bigger, though I wouldn't have thought he could.

Crap. Too late to look away.

My smile, I realized, *felt* sheepish at that point. And I didn't want to be a sheep with the way he was looking at me.

I felt a tugging at my skirt. I looked back to my lap. Minnie dangled from its denim hem. She snapped the fingers of her free hand. "Hey! Stop that!"

The wolf-kid glanced down now at Minnie, and the wolf-kid licked his chops. Minnie scaled my legs and disappeared into my open purse with a squeak.

Wolfie twitched, and I thought for a second he was going to lunge after Minnie. I flinched and pulled my bag closer to me. He snickered. I glared at him, drawing myself up just a bit, to show him that I stood head and shoulders taller than him. His grin retreated and he backed up a couple of inches.

Good. Nice to know I can be intimidating if I try, once in awhile.

My stop approached, so rather than have a prolonged staring contest, I reached up and behind me to pull the coated steel cord. The STOP REQUESTED sign lit up and dinged. Wolfie sighed and looked a lot more like a teenager than a predator. Was that a hint of apology in his eye? No matter, I hadn't seen him on this route before, maybe I wouldn't run into him again.

The bus slowed and stopped with a jerk at the next corner. I stood up before it came to a full stop and almost took a tumble. Wolfie grabbed my hand to steady me. *Hmm, a budding gentleman in wolf's clothing?* I favored him with a warmer smile as I made my way to the front and down the steps to the street. I thanked the driver.

I found myself a little further from my stop than I wanted to walk. I sighed and slung my bag over a shoulder, the contents rattling and squeaking.

"I'd have been in a lot less trouble if you'd just told me later, you know?" I scolded Minnie, who stayed in my bag for the moment.

"Hey! You were sitting next to a freakin' wolf, dearheart! You want to be Red Riding Hood or Grandma, hmm?" Minnie's voice was muffled, but she was close enough for me to hear.

"Sure, a wolf who's not old enough to shave in the real world, a wolf who'd look me straight in the boobs if we were face to face. Oooh, scary." The problem with intelligent discussions like this one of course, is that it not only feels like I'm arguing with myself, I really kind of am.

"Whatever. It's in my best interest to look out for you, Gigantor. And I don't tell you about half the goons I see on the bus, you know."

I let this sit for a moment, wondering what lurked on buses that could be worse than the sneering punks and stinky bums I'd run into sometimes. I don't often ride the bus tipsy. I wondered if IndyGo bus rides would be more entertaining if I did. Or whether I might think twice about riding.

I decided that for the moment, I didn't want to know. Say what you want about the bus, it gets around Indianapolis well enough when I don't want to have to beg rides from Stuart or my friends and co-workers. Growing up in Chicago, I never had to learn to drive, and so far, I'd done okay here too. Besides, cars have a lot of expenses that go with them, and I just didn't want to deal with all that.

I walked the better part of a mile along the side of the busy road, crossing once, and my Starbucks came into view. I pulled my cell phone from my hip pocket and saw that I was going to be about 15 minutes early, plenty of time to change into my uniform.

The silent walk made me think that either my tiny spirit self had a case of the sulks, or my buzz had worn off and I couldn't hear her anymore. I decided it'd be a bad idea to show up with vodka on my breath, but didn't want to waste the booze, so as I entered the cafe', I snuck the covered cup into the vast, dark recesses of my purse as I retrieved my bundle of folded clothes.

Daria winked at me from behind the counter as I made my way to the ladies' room. She was explaining the difference between an Americano and a regular decaf coffee to a couple of teen girls who didn't stop their texting to look up at her. Ah, customers.

In the women's room, I hung my bag on the hook of the stall and stepped out of my boots and skirt, and into my brown polyester slacks and boat shoes. My white polo shirt would do for a top so I just pulled the green apron on and tied it behind my back. As I put my boots and skirt into my big purse, I thought about the six-hour shift ahead of me and sighed. Like my speculation about drinking on the bus, I found myself wondering whether my shift would be more or less entertaining with booze.

I decided to play it safe and leave that as a thought experiment.

I stowed my purse upright under the counter, trying not to tip my cup inside. I joined Daria and Theo, my fellow baristas, with a smile. Daria let me take the next counter customer while she concocted something full of whipped cream and chocolate.

It's not a bad job, and I think we get a ton more respect than fast food workers. My personal point of pride is that silly title... barista. It sounds exotic, foreign, and people say it with a bit of the respect they'd use to talk about their bartender. Well, that's how I see it anyway, it helps me get through my shifts.

Besides, I get to work with some pretty cool folks.

Daria's short, round and adorable. I just want to take her home and keep her with my plushie collection sometimes. She tries to cover up the cute with her raunchy sense of humor, but it just makes me want to pinch her cherub-like cheeks and make coochy-coo noises over her. She pretends to hate that about me, but I can tell by the little flush to her cheeks that deep down she likes it.

Theo's whip-wiry and nerdy. I can't help but think of Urkel when he greets me with his goofy grin. He'll never know of my super-secret childhood crush on Jaleel White. I mourned when I found out that the show had been in reruns and our age difference would be too great to ignore. *Le sigh*.

I love nerdy guys. I'm not sure why. I just always have adored a guy who comes out of his shell to show his smarts. Besides, they're easy to butter up. Taller girls won't look at 'em twice, wanting some big bear of a man to make them feel small by comparison. Not me.

Like Stuart. I met him when we both lived in Chicago, our first romance started in-character in a live-action role-playing game. I was like Morticia to his Gomez. Everyone but us saw through the transparent act before we did, and we found ourselves dating outside of the game as well as in.

So, when he got a job down here in Indiana, I gave up my last ties to the Windy City and followed him.

A customer said my name. It might not have been the first time. I'd been daydreaming. It always irks me when someone uses my nametag against me. It's even still got the "funny" typo, saying "Skyy" like the vodka. Monica kept promising I'd get a new name-tag when everyone did when the next uniform order came in. Meanwhile I had to put up with all the amused comments from customers who think they're the first person ever to crack a joke about wanting some of that in their coffee.

Ha. Me too, sweeties.

After covering for my lapse, most of my shift sped by. I caught a few odd things out of the corner of my eye, a grotesque shadow where it shouldn't be, a distorted reflection of something supernatural for an instant before a blink of my eyes restored them to a businesswoman or a professor-type or a gaggle of kids.

That happens with my second sight. It can be unpredictable, showing me glimpses and peeks into the shadow world when I'm paying the least attention. Most of all when I'm tired or distracted.

I didn't get any more frantic warnings from Minnie, at least, so I felt pretty safe. Indy seemed a lot safer in general that way. Up in Chicago, I'd had glimpses of nightmares that I don't care to recall even in broad daylight. Not that Chicago's a bad place... it was my home for most of my life, after all, and it'll always be a part of me. But it's a bigger, tougher place than Indy, and I think more things hide in a crowd up there than down here.

Plus, it was where I met the demon. Brrr, let's not think about that right now. Later.

Toward the end of my shift, the crowd slowed down for dinnertime. They'd be back in force after a full meal for evening meet-ups. Daria left for home as Monica arrived to preside over the evening shift. I was tending the thin stream of commuter customers, cleaning as I went so that I'd be able to leave on time. Monica's kind of a hard-ass about that, she's been known to make someone work after clocking out because they didn't clean their station to her satisfaction. She's not a tyrant, but it's obvious my stocky manager enjoys what power she wields.

"MacLeod, here comes your man," said Monica, her tone holding an unspoken warning.

"Stuart? Mon, I worked through my break, can I please just go say hi?"

Monica sighed and nodded. "Go. Just take off the apron while you're on break, okay?"

I let out a happy noise and gave her a quick hug. It was like hugging a mannequin. I guess I should have known hugs are wasted on Monica, but what can I say? I'm a hugger. I gave Theo a quick hug too since he was already moving to cover the next customer at the counter for me.

I glanced at the customer and got a sudden chill. On the surface, she was just another teen girl trying to look more grown up by buying high end coffee. With skin pale as sour cream, her shiny, bottle-black bobbed hair framed her face. She had cherry-stained pouty lips and enough eyeliner to make Johnny Depp jealous. Her deep purple stretchy velvet scoop-necked top fit her form in a way that made me think of sensuous fuzzy eggplants. I almost giggled.

I know her! People called her Queenie. A recent addition to our live-action Vampire game, she'd already risen above my rank in only a few weeks. I suspected her eggplants had something to do with it.

She was an odd one though; in a Vampire game, she chose to play a werewolf. Several of the younger guys had given up better ranks among the vamps to follow her around as her wolf pups.

I thought maybe she and Wolfie from the bus would get along just swell. For his sake, I kind of hoped they wouldn't meet. Queenie'd lead him around by the nose, and he'd do pretty much whatever she asked.

Now, I'm not above wanting that kind of attention, but Queenie hadn't done much for the game as a whole to deserve it, while I'd paid my dues and helped further plots and intrigue over the past year or so that I'd been in it. The thralls who sucked up to me, well, they were fun, but I didn't abuse the privilege. Not much, anyway.

She flicked her eyes up to meet mine and allowed her cherry lips to curve just a little. I thought of Elvis, and the comparison snapped me out of it. I smiled back and made a tiny bow to show I remembered her from the game. She didn't acknowledge me though; she transfixed poor little Theo with a hundred-watt smile.

"Hell-o?" Stuart was at the end of the counter, waving a hand slowly in the air to get my attention. Right, Stuart. I pulled the apron over my head and tossed it on my bag and skipped over to him, kissing the top of his head.

"Aren't you sweet, stopping by after getting off work?"

Stuart tilted his head up to kiss me on the lips, just a quick little peck. I'm sure he just didn't want to get me in trouble with the boss. He took my hand and led me over to a couch so we could sit together for a few minutes.

"Figured you'd appreciate a ride," he began, his cute pudgy butt sinking into the soft leather couch. I plopped down next to him, making him pop up as the cushion plumped up. I laughed as he grabbed the arm of the couch to steady himself. He sighed.

"So, does this mean we can finally go Goodwill hunting?" I was pushing my luck. Stuart hates shopping, clothes shopping in particular. You'd think just getting to see me model them would be incentive enough. Well, a girl can hope, can't she?

"Well... I've got a raid online later I've got to run..." he began, a bit of a whine in his voice.

I matched him whine for whine, hamming it up. "But Stewieee," he hates when I call him Stewie. "The Danse Macabre is Saturday! I need to get a dress, and I need time to alter it. You know, to bring the sexy to the par-tay!" I waggled my eyebrows, hoping this would add spice to the pot.

Stuart sighed. "If you can make it quick, we can go..."

He didn't get to finish, because I pounce-hugged him. "Thank you, baby! I knew I meant more to you than killing orcs with nerds you've never met!"

Stuart laughed and hugged me back. "You talk like you've never played Warcraft with me, Miss Night Elf Paladin."

Sure I've played. I play a couple times a week. I have fun at it too. But with Stuart, it's easier to count the hours of his free time he's not glued to the computer doing raids over and over. I decided not to go there, though, since I know when to quit when I'm ahead. Sometimes.

I thanked him with a few more kisses, making him give me a bit more than a peck. I liked that I could melt him like this.

All too soon, my break was over, and sighed as Monica tapped an imaginary watch on her wrist. I left Stuart there and fetched my apron. My bag started to tip, and I thought of the booze and caught it in time and made sure it sat upright.

I smiled and greeted my next customer, a cute little old man with a rumpled hat. Behind him, a shadow seemed to pass over the sun outside, as though night had fallen all at once.

I looked away from the man to see better, but now all I saw was daylight. *I am seeing things or is Minnie up to something? No way. She'd never been able to do anything quite that impressive to get my attention.*

The little old man looked around to follow my gaze. His eyes locked onto Queenie, who slutted her way to the door. He smiled and looked back at me and said, "Sweetheart, I've seen the type, she's trouble."

I started to ask him what he meant when she opened the door. The glass all around still showed the daytime parking lot, but within the frame of the open door, it was a nighttime forest, a full moon hanging in the sky.

I'm sure I must have gaped. I know I had to close my mouth after the door shut.

The old guy made another remark, but I didn't hear him. I was too preoccupied as I watched my boyfriend follow Queenie out.

Chapter Two

I started to run around the counter after Stuart, but Monica stopped me with a hand on my shoulder. Sure, now she decides that touching is okay.

"Hey," she said, "Where are you going? You still have another half hour, and you've got a customer!"

"Mon, I've got to follow Stu, he's..." I scrambled for excuses. I said, "He's my ride!" It sounded lame, even to me.

"Skye... I don't care, you've got a half hour to go, and you take the bus most days, so this can be another one of those days." She tried to steer me back to the old guy. Theo was already covering for me, bless him.

"I can't explain, but it's really important to me, an *emergency*, Mon."

Monica studied my face and hesitated a moment. Then she shook her head. "No. Sorry. If you go, then you may as well not come back. I'm sorry, Skye."

My mind raced. Why would Stuart follow Queenie? What was going on with that forest I saw? Maybe Stuart was in danger.

I burst into tears. I hate even admitting it happened, and it was made all the worse that it happened in front of Monica and Theo, the old guy and the other customers. I knew everyone was looking at me. I wiped at my tears, but more kept flowing as the frustration welled up inside me.

Monica took her hand off my shoulder and stepped out of my way. "Oh for God's sake, MacLeod, pull yourself together. Fine, whatever, just go. I can't have you making a scene here."

I blubbered something incomprehensible at Monica and grabbed for my purse. I fumbled it, and it fell sideways on the floor. The cup burst open and sprayed vodka-water all over the floor. There was a loud metal clanking as my flask slid out and spun on the floor between Monica and me.

The Starbucks went silent as I looked up from collecting my stuff, finding my manager's hard glare focused on me.

"You're fired, Skye."

"But…" I began, pleading.

"No. You know the policy on alcohol at Starbucks. If I don't fire you, I'd be fired myself. Leave the apron. Get out. You can come by Friday for your last check. I'm sorry."

I threw the apron in the puddle and stuffed my flask in my purse and didn't look back as I rounded the counter. I didn't want to see Monica's glare. I didn't want to see pity in Theo's eyes.

The old guy called after me, but I didn't hear as I pulled the door open. I walked out into the parking lot, not into a moonlit forest. I ran past the cars and called out Stuart's name, but although his car was still in the lot, he and Queenie were nowhere to be seen. I was alone with the cars and the heat haze of the blacktop.

I looked up and down the street, still wiping at the drying tears on my face with a sleeve. I couldn't deal with being fired just now, the panic rising in me as Stuart's sudden disappearance sunk in.

I pulled out my cell phone and called his number. It rang and rang and paused, and for a second, I held my breath, thinking he'd picked up, but it was his voicemail.

"Stuart," I said into the phone, "I don't know where you went. I'm outside Starbucks… um, your car's here, but… well, I saw you leave and you're not out here now. Please call me, sweetie, I'm worried."

I sat on the back bumper of his old black Taurus and thought about my options. I could wait here, but I felt embarrassed enough to have been fired for something so stupid and for crying in front of everyone. I was sure people inside could see me. I could go home on my own, on the bus, and wait for him. I could imagine myself there, eating myself from the inside, dying for my cell phone to ring, the door to open.

I needed another perspective, and I needed to calm down. Freaking out like this didn't do anyone any good. So, I took a walk around behind the coffee shop and took a long drink from my flask. I fought a feeling of heavy shame, but I needed Minnie. And maybe I'd see some doorway to wherever Stuart might be.

As the alcohol spread out through my body, it warmed me. I appreciated the light evening breeze that wafted past, cooling me as it dried the misting of sweat on my skin.

I drank another long drink, and another. I shook the flask from side to side and felt not too much left inside, so I capped it and put it away. I took a deep breath and felt tingly and calmer. *Take this job and shove it,* I thought to myself.

A slow clapping came from inside my purse, and Minnie popped her tousled head out to smirk at me. "Bra-vo, babe. You are like, the awesomest."

Fury burned inside me, wrecking the calm the booze had begun to build. "Yeah? So what, I should have let my man get abducted to Fairyland so I could keep my job? I should have left my flask at home? I'm thinking maybe that'd be best, I wouldn't be taking abuse from my mini-me if I had!" I was tempted to shake the purse, but I'm not a mean drunk.

Minnie's expression fell. "Hey, hey! I'm on your side, sister! I can't help but be! It just wasn't our most shining moment, hmm? I just meant you sure know how to make an exit, is all. What happened, anyway, I was, um, napping, at least until you dumped the bag all over the floor."

I explained to her about the moonlit forest doorway Queenie had gone through, and seeing Stuart disappear. She looked surprised.

"Wow, that's some serious mojo right there. Did you know there was something about that chick?"

I shrugged. "She's a big deal in the game, has guys eating out of her hand. Literally. I thought I caught scraps of some kind of aura around her, but I've never been under the influence in her presence, so nothing reliable."

Minnie frowned. "That kind of wattage should be visible from space, ya know?"

I shrugged. "So do you think Stu's in danger?"

Minnie hesitated, then nodded. "He could be. Depends on how much the game means to her, I guess. If she really wants to keep her cushy spot and her followers, then messing with Stuart isn't smart, since he's well known, and influential. Plus, she had to have seen you chewing on his face on the sofa, so doing that right in front of you left a witness. Sure, no one'll believe you, but she's got to know you're gonna look for him."

I thought about it for a bit before saying anything more. Queenie... what the hell was her real name, anyway? She did seem to enjoy the hell out of the attention she got in game. And it would be a lot of time wasted if she couldn't show her face around the club again, after making Stuart disappear. "Yeah, okay, that makes sense, he's pretty much got to be okay,"

I noticed a swarm of tiny twig-men skittering around the corner. They were fighting over a half-eaten carrot cake muffin, likely pilfered from the trash. I pointed, and Minnie giggled. "Aww, ain't they adorable?"

I had to agree. Each was a tiny cluster of animated twigs and sticks, like miniature models of Ents from Lord of the Rings put together by a child. They didn't belong here. "Hey. Go ask them what they know, would you, Min?"

She shrugged and I eased my purse to the ground. Minnie scrambled out onto the pavement and walked over to the half dozen or so twig-men and asked, "Sup, twiggies?"

The little figures froze and whispered among themselves. They formed a defensive ring around the muffin fragment and scrambled away to the front side of the store.

"They ain't talkers," said Minnie, climbing back onto my purse, hanging onto the strap with one hand as I replaced it on my shoulder with care.

"What do you think their deal is?"

"Bet they came through that door when it was open."

I sighed. "So where's the door now? Where's Stuart?"

Minnie patted my elbow with her little hand. "Okay, so how's this? I'll see what I can find out. You need to get outta here. I don't think that door's coming back unless Queenie herself opens it. You know, maybe it was even a mistake that Stuart made it through."

Right. "Yeah, a mistake. He *followed* her, Minnie. What's that all about, huh? One minute, he's all sweet, coming to pick me up and take me shopping, then before you know it, he's tailing Queen Bitch!"

Just then, Monica came around the corner. I was too startled to say anything, so I waited for her to come to me.

"Hey," she said, poker-faced.

"Hey," I replied. I'd be damned if I was going to lead this conversation. Whatever it turned out to be about.

Monica couldn't meet my eyes, looking around. Maybe the Dumpster was just too fascinating. "A customer said he'd seen you still hanging around."

I shrugged. "It's still a free country, unless you're going to tell me I'm trespassing."

She shook her head. We made eye contact for only a second, then she looked away. "I'm sorry it had to be like that, Skye," she said.

"Rules is rules," I said in a bland tone.

She nodded. "Yeah, they are. But I'm still not happy it had to end that way."

"Imagine how I feel," I said, my voice caught in my throat. *No crying, Skye. Not in front of her.*

Monica paused, then said, "Okay, have it your way. I'll see you around. If you need a reference, I'll give you a good one. I'll leave out the circumstances of your termination. Okay?"

I'm sure I should have been more cordial, but the booze made me say, "Whatever helps you sleep at night, Mon."

Her eyes hardened, and she nodded and turned and left without another word.

"Like I said, you gotta get outta here," said Minnie as my former employer rounded the corner to go back inside.

I looked at my cell phone. I could catch a bus in 15 minutes, or I could call Stuart again. Or...

"Maybe I should call someone else," I began.

"Call Leslie," my tiny alter-ego commanded.

I nodded and did as she said.

"Yo, Blue Skye, what's up?" Leslie rumbled from his end of the line.

"Hey, Les, I'm kinda in a bind. Can you give me a ride? Stuart's... well, he's flaked out on me, and the Danse Macabre is this weekend..."

"Hon, I'm way ahead of you. Wait til you see what I found for you, it's not gonna take much alteration, either. Where are you?"

"Oh Les, you're my hero! Pick me up at... work?" I decided not to tell him everything just yet.

"Sure, be right there, darlin'." and he ended the call.

I waited there behind the building until I heard the low rumble of Leslie's motorcycle. I walked out into the lot, and the sight of him washed my worries away.

Leslie's a big bear of a man, and he takes the teasing he gets for resembling the Hogwarts groundskeeper, Hagrid, with good grace. I've yet to discover whether he's gay, straight or something else, since I've never seen him more passionate about a person than he is about cosplay. He'd only come to Indy last winter when Stuart found him a new day job, but he was already beloved by the vampires as costumer and makeup artist. More than that, he'd never met a stranger, and he took care of people. I only wish I could be that content and loved by so many.

He unsnapped a helmet from the back of his bike and handed it to me. It was adorned with Hello Kitty and despite my troubles, I squealed like a little girl.

"Leslie, did you get this just for me, or is it for all the girls?"

He chuckled, adding more bass to the engine's stutter. "You're the only one for me, Skye Blue. You and all the other girls, of course."

I pouted for a second or two, as long as I could hold back my grin. "I should know better than to ask." I put on the super cute helmet and climbed on behind my big friend and hugged myself to him. It was a comfort I needed, and I felt embarrassment melt away from me as we roared out of the parking lot. I guess I do know how to make an exit after all.

Leslie lives in Broad Ripple, just up the Monon Rail Trail from where Stuart and I live. He took a longer way around, parading us down the main drag of Broad Ripple like he was showing me off. Showing himself off, maybe. People did look at us, but Leslie wasn't the only one who wanted to show off, and this was the place to do it. He revved the engine, and I didn't hold my smile back as I got jealous stares from some of the girls on the sidewalk.

Among the beautiful people were a few faint other things, often overlaid like a ghost over a human body. On one side was a stereotypical frat guy, but if I squinted just right, I could see goat legs on him, like a satyr. On the other was a swanky businesswoman in a pencil skirt and heels, her huge black-feathered wings spread out behind her. The buzz must be fading a bit if they looked so translucent to me. Still, I saw more than anyone else, both my blessing and my curse.

Also, there were couples, some holding hands, and that made me think of my Stuart, spirited away to who knows where by whoever she really was. A wicked fairy queen, perhaps, dabbling in the lives of mortals. I shivered. No one but me could say that with a straight face, and so there was no use telling anyone. All I could do is wait and hope.

Leslie pulled off the main drag and followed the back streets to his apartment building. He swung his sputtering motorcycle into a carport and killed the engine. I hopped off, realizing too late that it was a good thing I hadn't had a chance to change back into my little denim skirt. Leslie swung a massive leg over the seat and led me by the hand back to his place. I suppose there's something to a guy who can make even a willowy girl feel small, on occasion.

Leslie's place wasn't glamorous like you'd expect from a creative guy like him. He lives for the fantasy world we create among us, not the real world. He just stored stuff at his place, and he slept and worked his mortal magic there. With imagination, he could build kingdoms, dress others like royalty, and fulfill the dark fantasies of others with a little paint, lacquer, some leather and some lace.

It almost made me curious about Leslie, what that kind of passion and imagination might be like between the sheets. I rejected the thought as soon as it came; that'd be just about like incest. Leslie was my friend, my big brother in spirit. I decided it'd be better just to imagine he didn't swing my way.

Maybe that's why I never see Leslie with anyone.

He let go my hand at the door and let us inside. His living room was cluttered with a maze of stacked plastic storage bins, dressmaker's dummies and a clothing rack. An elderly brown sofa and a couple of scruffy orange armchairs were pushed off onto one wall. A small computer desk with a monitor sat in another corner. Leslie didn't own a TV.

My large friend gestured that I should sit, and wound his own way to the entrance to the apartment's kitchen. I heard the fridge open and shut, followed by a couple of clinking noises. Leslie returned with a couple of beers, and earned himself the honor of Skye's Favorite Person of the Day by handing me one. The bottle had no markings, and I couldn't tell much about it through the dark brown glass. I looked up at him with a question on my face.

"It's one of Heath's private brews. Think this one's Cuckoo for Cocoa Porter, if I remember right. Cheers," he said, clinking his bottle against mine.

At this rate, he was going for Skye's Favorite Person of the Week. I echoed his toast and drank in the deep, dark, bittersweet home-brewed beer. Heath's skill as a brewer, both private and professional, was legendary among the vampire crowd. He'd created amazing beer and meads, using spices and ingredients you wouldn't expect to taste good together. He claimed some of them to be "medicinal" like that strange ginger mead he'd made. It had been so strong in ginger flavor that I felt like I was drinking Mentholatum. It had a burn to it, but it was a good burning, and it even cleared up a cold I'd had coming on.

Heath's cocoa porter turned out to have a strong aroma and aftertaste of dark chocolate. *Oh, heaven!* Before I knew it, I'd drank half of the strong beer, and I'd sunk deep into Leslie's elderly orange chair. My problems seemed distant, and I felt at ease.

Leslie sipped at his beer and fussed around the room. The sight of a fussy giant was pretty damned amusing to me. I heard a stirring in my purse, and as I looked over, Minnie slipped out and climbed up to sit on the arm of my chair. I showed her the bottle and raised my eyebrows, but she shook her head and smiled at me.

"So," Leslie said, pausing before going on, "What's with your man? How'd he flake out this time? Forget to pick you up because he's on a raid? Too much porn?"

I snorted, in the middle of another swig of beer, which caused me to cough. Lucky for me, it didn't come out my nose. I held up a finger until I could speak. "Not this time, but he did wander off after promising me a ride and a shopping trip. Left his car and everything."

Minnie waved her little hands in warning, and I ignored her. I hadn't told Leslie anything about my second sight so far, and I didn't plan on changing that anytime soon. The last thing I needed was to weird out one of my best friends. It's bad enough that Stuart never believed me about the things I'd seen.

Maybe he would now!

"Hmm," rumbled Leslie. "Stu's always been good to you since you hooked up, but he's lost track of reality if he's stood you up like that."

I was caught in mid-swig again, but managed not to choke on that swallow, despite being struck funny by the irony. "Yeah, I know.... It does seem kind of out there for him. I'm worried about him, to be honest; I'm not sure where he went. I left him a message. I guess he'll call when he's back." I hoped.

Leslie grunted. "Yeah, probably. So, do you wanna see what I found?"

Oh! The dress! Minnie had to duck to keep her perch as I put my arms up in a "Y" and squealed. "Show me, show me, show me!"

He allowed himself a little smile and turned to paw through the clothes rack. He selected a hanger and revealed a dress with a flourish.

Oh pretty!

Leslie held up a medium-length sheath of shiny red satin, cut in a Mandarin style, with a high neck and a slit up each side. Tiny buttons covered with the same cloth adorned one shoulder and fastened along the left of the front panel of the dress.

I set the almost empty bottle down on the floor and leaped up to take the garment from him and held it up in front of me. I don't know how he does it, but it looked like it'd fit me.

"Oh my God, Leslie, where did you find this?" I was in love with the dress already. The cloth felt cool and slick against me.

"Hmm, trade secret, but it's from a thrift store, so I got it for a song. Try it on. 'Sides, there's a water mark staining the right side there in front. I'll do something to cover it."

I stumbled once as I wove my way through the tubs and bric-a-brac in the living room on my way to the bathroom. I'd changed in front of him before, since his van was also the changing room for the Vampire game. Since we were alone in his apartment, I felt a little modesty was appropriate.

The dress fit like an erotic dream. I felt slinky, sexy, and wicked wearing it. I left my Starbucks clothes, boots and purse in a heap on the bathroom floor and padded out in bare feet to show him.

Leslie nodded his approval. "Perfect. You'll be the Dame of the Danse, Skye. I'll find some stuff to go with it, and we can improvise on your makeup, but I'm thinking 'China Doll' or something similar."

I hugged him, loving the feel of the slippery dress pressed between us. I kissed his cheek and he coughed and patted my back. "Glad you like it," he remarked. "Gotta leave it here for now so I can work on it some more, though."

I changed back, and after I had another couple of beers (Leslie only had the one), I asked him to take me back to my place. Maybe something was wrong with Stuart's phone, so I should go home and look for him. Also, if I spent much more time here, I'd want to move in.

I decided we should walk back since it was only a few blocks down the Monon Trail. The converted rail line was the shortest path from his place to ours, but since it's not lit, the gloom of late evening was spooky. I walked close to Leslie, since the beer had my second sight revealing all sorts of shadowy figures hunching their way along the side of the path, the glowing embers of their eyes flashing as they watched us pass by. I shivered. Leslie peered at me through the twilight. "Had too much?" he asked.

I shook my head. "I've had just enough. The dark can be a little freaky...." I made something up. "You hear about attacks along the Monon at night, that's why it's supposed to be closed at dusk, officially."

He studied me a moment longer, then nodded. "Sure, got it."

I tried to keep my eyes straight ahead of me, but even still, I heard scrabbling of something on the pavement behind us. Claws? Talons? Best not to know, I thought. Keep cool, Skye. Nothing's gonna mess with Leslie.

But could he fight what he didn't even see or hear?

Relief came as we reached the cross street that led to Stuart's house. The dark windows said that he wasn't home yet, and I didn't see his car parked along the side of the street. My heart sank a little.

Leslie took me to my door, and waited while I undid the lock, opened the door, and turned on the lights inside. "You can either swing by my place before the Danse or I'll have the dress with me when I get there, 'k?"

I smiled at him and nodded. "Thanks so much for everything, you big galoot," I said, aware somewhere inside that I was acting too affectionate for his comfort. *It's the beer.* I reached over and mussed up his helmet-head hair, then leaned over and kissed him on the cheek again. He steadied me as I lost my balance, and used the opportunity to take a step back after.

"Night, Starry Skye, be good," he said as he turned and slouched his way back toward the Monon.

I shut the door and bolted it. I thought I'd be looking forward to a long night of worry, but just then, my phone rang.

Stuart!

I fumbled the phone in my haste to answer it. I had to scramble on all fours on the floor to chase after it. I punched the "talk" button even without picking it up off the carpet and pressed my face against it.

"Hey babe," he said, his voice shaky and thin.

I felt like laughing with relief as I heard his voice. "Are you okay, Stewie?"

"Yeah. I'm... I'm torn up a bit, but I'm okay." I could hear the turn signal clicking, so I knew he was in his car, driving.

"Torn up? Are you on your way home?"

"Yeah. Almost there. Didn't get a chance to call until now. I'll tell you when I get there, okay? Don't freak out."

What else could I say? "I'll be waiting, love."

I didn't want to hang up, I wanted to keep him on the line until I could see him, but he cut the call.

I picked up my phone and pocketed it. Soon enough, I heard his key in the lock, and I cursed myself for locking it. I turned the bolt from my side, and pulled the door open, dragging his keys from his hand as they stayed in the lock.

He was a mess. I could see blood soaking his jeans where they were torn. His shirt was ripped in straight parallel lines, and it was streaked with blood. Like claw marks.

Chapter Three

I helped Stuart out of his shredded clothing and fussed over him. I couldn't get him to talk about what happened, he just repeated that he was tired. He shied away from my touch, but he was too weak to enforce his protests.

I towed him into the bathroom. I ran hot water in the sink, and I pumped some antibacterial soap into it as it filled. Stuart sat slumped and bloody on the toilet as I got out a fresh washcloth and soaked it in the warm, foamy water. I wrung it out and dabbed at his wounds.

As I dabbed, the blood came off, but I found no wounds underneath, only pink lines of scar tissue. The skin around the scars looked red and angry, but none of it was broken or torn like I expected. In fact, I found no open wounds at all on him to have made all the blood. I didn't know what to think. Where, or who, did the blood come from? How could his clothes have gotten so ripped and blood-soaked?

Why doesn't he answer me?

Stuart nodded off a few times while I tended to him, and I had to keep one hand on him to keep him from slumping right off his seat. When I was done, I dragged him to his feet against his piteous complaints. Getting him upstairs to our bed was out of the question. I led him to the living room and plunked him on the couch. I fetched shorts and a too-large game convention shirt from years ago. He complained more as I dressed him for sleep, but looked peaceful once I'd gotten him arranged, laid out on the couch. His snoring began right away; the familiar rhythmic roar calmed me.

Except, I couldn't afford to be calm. Something had attacked my boyfriend, and even without obvious wounds, my man had returned to me drained, maybe traumatized. I needed to stay awake and watch over him, in case something came for him.

At least I can sleep in tomorrow, one plus of being unemployed.

I'd have to have all my senses open, which meant maintaining a buzz. I went to the kitchen and rummaged through the liquor cupboard and came up with half a bottle of spiced rum. That'd do. I found most of a two-liter of diet generic cola in the fridge. Even better. I mixed the two in roughly equal measures over ice in a cheap plastic stadium cup from a pizza place nearby. The soda didn't fizz much as it hit the ice, but I found a green plastic lime with some juice left in the door. *Perfect.* I added a squirt of lime and called it a Cuba Libre. It tasted pretty good, even flat.

I took my drink out into the living room. Stuart still snored away, sleeping the sleep of the dead. The thought chilled me. It occurred to me that I'd just about lost him tonight, and I still had no idea why.

The alcohol and caffeine battled within me as I sipped at my Cuba Libre, a pleasant feeling. This internal chemical struggle kept me alert for awhile, but with nothing going on, loosening up threatened to segue into sleep.

I have to get up and do something.

I paced up and down awhile. I killed some time by fetching some more comfortable clothing, a long, light, olive-colored hippie-style skirt and a matching baby doll T-shirt. I felt like I needed to be ready for anything, so I kept on some sturdy sandals. Bored, I painted my toenails a dark coppery red.

At last, finding nothing else to keep me awake, I gravitated to Stuart's computer in the living room, where I could keep watch. I set the stadium cup on the desk, clicked on the flat panel monitor and took another generous gulp of my drink.

He'd left his PC on earlier, and I found several views into women's bedrooms in various windows. I sighed and glared at Stuart's inert body with imaginary laser beams shooting from my eyes. We went around and around about this, and had for years. He loved being a voyeur; he watched web-streaming video of exhibitionist women as they lived their lives. I hated it. He said it wasn't porn; it was just a fascination with peering into other people's lives. He never had a good answer when I asked why he didn't 'peer in' on any men, if there wasn't anything sexual about it.

The closest answer he ever had was pointing out that "Babette" included her man, "Raoul", in her broadcasts. We'd met them a couple of years ago, by chance, at a paranormal convention in Chicago. They'd been mixed up in some trouble, and we'd helped them. That was when it had begun, my second sight. *When the demon had come.* As always, I pushed that thought aside. It was how I'd gained my second sight, and Minnie, but that night was not one I cared to remember.

I checked and found Babette and Raoul cuddled up on a couch, watching TV in their Memphis apartment. They'd made some news last year, and their web show about ghost hunting was doing well as a result.

I closed the other video windows in irritation, but hesitated over them. I remembered being tangled up with Raoul after he ran into me in the dark. Mmm, he was pretty yummy for an older guy. I enlarged the window, watching them awhile. I sighed, wishing I were in that calm, loving scene instead of the stressful day and night I'd had. Raoul looked happy with Babette's head in his lap. He stroked her spiky black hair with obvious affection. She smiled too, enjoying herself.

Stuart's a full subscriber to Babette's webcam site, so the window had a chat box hanging off the bottom. I don't know why, but I typed in "hey there". There must be an alert on the other end, because Babette bounced up off of Raoul's lap and peered out of the screen at me.

She couldn't see me, so I guessed she thought I was Stuart as she typed back, "Hey! What are you doing up?"

I thought about toying with her, seeing how far her friendship with Stuart went, but overcame the booze's influence. I trust Stuart. And I like Babette, she was good to me after the demon... well, she helped, anyway.

I typed back, "Hey, it's Skye. Stuart was attacked and I'm staying up to make sure he stays safe."

Concern flooded over her features, and I saw her call over her shoulder. Raoul joined her at the desk, reading what I'd written.

We went back and forth in text conversation as I filled them in on what I knew and what I didn't know. I told them about the lack of wounds, despite the blood on his clothes and skin. After a few exchanges, I received a video chat invitation, which I accepted.

I saw myself appear in the corner of the video stream, and I have to say, I looked a lot better than I felt.

They smiled as they saw me, and her squeaky voice made me smile in return as she greeted me. "Hey girl! I gotta ask, have you *seen* anything?"

These two continue to be friends of mine because they are among the select few who are willing to believe me when I talk about what I see with my second sight. They were there to pick me up after the demon had left me laying there on the beach, and they'd performed the ritual that kept my soul from leaking out after the possession. Raoul himself had been possessed, and was in a more advanced state of leakage when I'd met him. Minnie was that bit of me that'd leaked out, and she'd become my shadow from then on.

So, I decided to trust them and told them about Queenie and the door into the moonlit forest, and how he'd been gone for hours before reappearing. They listened with serious expressions, not doubting me at all. It felt good to tell someone.

"So, I'm keeping myself a little lit as I sit up. I haven't seen anything in our place so far. I don't think they like to enter uninvited, but I'm not taking chances."

Babette nodded. "Skye, just be careful, don't drink so much that you'll be worthless if something does happen. I've got a bad feeling about all this. I don't want to scare you, but you'd better get some things together, a sort of spiritual self-defense kit." Raoul nodded his agreement.

"Like what? Keep booze handy, sure, but what can I do against fairies?"

Babette giggled at this. "Fairies, hmm? Well, they're more than that, but I get what you mean. Remember this: silver is your best defense against the supernatural, but cold iron is your best offense. Also, keep something personal on you, maybe something that's important to both of you."

I held up a finger and ran upstairs and rummaged through my jewelry box and grabbed a few things.

I showed them what I'd gotten. First, a couple of silver rings, one in a Celtic knot style, the other a spinner ring, its outer ring decorated with a metal daisy chain. Babette nodded her approval as I put these on, one on each hand.

Next, I held up a wrought iron tavern puzzle. My dad had given it to me before he died. It was a couple of little horseshoes linked by rings. Babette suggested something longer, so I wouldn't have to get so close if there was fighting. I searched the room and brought back an iron fireplace poker. Babette clapped and grinned her approval

Last, I held up a pendant. It was a micro-SD chip, embedded in resin, dangling from a silver-plated ball chain necklace. When they asked about it, I explained. "Stuart gave it to me late last year, after we'd been living together here in Indy for a year. It's a chip that has all our old chat logs on it, from when we first met. It's best that it's encased in resin, because some of it is pretty racy!"

I winked at the screen, looking at Raoul, though I doubted they could tell. He colored a little red anyway, which I thought was *adorable*.

Babette winked at me and said, "That's great, Skye. Keep that on you, it's something to hang onto if that Queenie has any more tricks up her sleeve. Think of it as a magic amulet, the soul of your relationship with Stuart, if you will."

I liked how she thought. I snapped the chain around my neck and offered them a view of it dangling in my cleavage. Raoul stayed pink in the cheeks and Babette just dimpled.

"You should start your own webcam site, darlin'," she drawled. "Showing off like that, you'll have a following in no time."

I sat back in my chair and stuck my tongue out at her. "No offense, but I don't want just anyone looking down my blouse."

"We're special, then?" said Raoul with his tone much dryer than the story his face told.

I flashed him my most winning smile.

Babette blew me a kiss. "Thanks, sweetie. Good luck with your fairy problem, but it's getting past our bedtime, and this movie's not gonna watch itself, you know?"

I nodded, finding myself sad that they had to go. "Okay. Any advice on staying up late?"

Raoul nodded. "Games. Play games on the computer. Anything to keep your mind active."

After they signed off, I watched them cuddle up on their couch at their place down in Memphis. I watched until I started to feel drowsy.

I stood up and paced around, sipping my drink. I peered out the window into the dark summer night. I'm not sure if I was more relieved or anxious when I failed to see any glowing eyes peering back at me.

After checking on Stuart for the tenth time in as many minutes, I took Raoul's advice and started up a game. If I have a secret vice, it's The Sims. If Stuart loves peeping in on real women, I love watching the lives of my little simulated family unfold, their tiny cartoon selves unaware of my godlike influence as I click them and make decisions for them.

It's a rush sometimes, messing with their tiny little lives. Yes, you may go to the bathroom. No, you may not get something to eat. I want you to flirt with the neighbor some more. Oh yes, please *do* kiss each other...

I reached the bottom of my Cuba Libre and was sad. I wandered into the kitchen to refresh it. While I was down there getting the last of the rum, I grabbed an unopened plastic bottle of vodka. Before resuming my (mostly) benevolent manipulation of my Sims, I slipped the bottle in my big purse. Babette said I should be ready for anything, right?

I ran my little simulated people through another week. I was passed buzzed and on into the stage where the room was swimming around me. I held onto the mouse a little tighter in hopes of slowing the spinning. I had the mother Sim reach her goal of becoming an Olympic medalist (bronze, oh well) when she looked right at me. The screen zoomed in until her perfect computer-generated face filled the computer screen. She spoke, this time in clear English, not the gibberish Simlish they babble throughout the game.

She said, "Skye, they're coming for you. Get help!"

I pushed myself away from the computer in shock, the rolling chair taking me a few feet away. My drink tipped over, so I lunged for it, hoping to prevent it from drenching the papers on the desk or frying the computer itself.

The screen was back to normal, mama Sim was in her red sports car, driving the streets of the imaginary town back to her home and family.

I'm so tired that I'm seeing things. More things.

I started to take another drink, but found the limey-spicy aroma turned my stomach just a bit now as the room did a dizzy, slow barrel roll around me.

I shut down the game. I peeked at the lone video stream, the empty couch in Memphis was dark and lonesome without my friends. I sighed and turned off the monitor.

Stuart still snored, the door was still locked and bolted, no wicked fairies peered in the windows at me. The quiet, spinning room allied with sleep, winning its war against the caffeine and my efforts to stay awake.

Before going to bed, I resolved to set my defenses. I grabbed a wrought iron poker and wielded it like a sword, making invisible "S"es in the air in front of me. I imagined myself to be a fierce Scottish warrior, like in the old family yarns Mom had told me when I was little.

Ha! Face the wrath of Skye MacLeod, fairy scum! There can be only one!

I climbed the stairs and flopped down in bed, and didn't even bother to take off my clothes. My poker and purse lay at the ready by my side where Stuart should have been. My last thoughts were that I hadn't seen Minnie since Leslie's place. Before the room did very many spins around me, sleep washed over me, taking me away from this world and into another.

I saw myself trotting along in the dark on the Monon. Except I looked much too short and the trail looked as wide as a six-lane highway, the trees on either side as tall as redwoods. *That's not me, that's my Minnie!* She stopped and spoke with some spindly, shadowy figures with hot coals for eyes. I couldn't hear what anyone said, there seemed to be music overpowering any sound. Something familiar and instrumental, but I couldn't recall just now.

The creature Minnie spoke to shook its head, then pointed back behind her and ran off, melting into the trees. Minnie turned, and I could see that an enormous, terrible woman was bearing down on her, letting out a screech as she clomped down some kind of metal basket over Minnie. A cage! Queenie had captured Minnie!

My view in the dream panned back, and Minnie clung to the side of the cage as it swung back and forth in Queenie's grip. Things blurred as she walked, each step seemed to take her very much further than it should. It was like she was pinching space so that her strides were ten, twenty times longer than they should be. She stretch-stepped up the Monon trail, and then followed one bank of the Central Canal. Things blurred still more and Queenie walked the trails of a moonlit forest. My dream-eyes were adjusted to the dark to the point where the moonlight was enough to see detail in the trees and rocks along the trail.

Her pace slowed, each step began to take her less and less extra distance until she walked at a normal pace up a hill in the woods. She reached a circle of stones. It looked so familiar. *I've been there before!*

Queenie placed the cage containing my Minnie in the center of the stones and began to walk around the outside. I could see her towering up above, the bars of the cage passing between my point of view, now looking over Minnie's shoulder, following Queenie's pacing.

Around and around the wicked fairy walked, gesturing and speaking words I could not hear. A shimmering wall of iridescent light rose up and light brightened inside the ring of stones. Queenie waded through the light, leaving a trail of more solid light behind her, like a slinky humanoid comet. Sparks flew from her fingertips and exploded out from under her shoes as she stepped.

When I could no longer see the trees of the forest hilltop through the band of multicolored light, Queenie stepped into the circle and picked up Minnie's cage once again.

After a short while, the light died down, and Queenie stepped out into a busy street underground somewhere. A vast cave spread out, but torches and colorful lanterns and will-o-wisp glows lit a street of tents and hasty shacks, tables and blankets. It was a market of some kind; a bazaar.

Merchants of all descriptions hawked their wares. I still couldn't hear them, but I now recognized the music as "In the Hall of the Mountain King" from Peer Gynt. Some creatures were large and hunched; others were tiny and quick. Some had wings, others claws and fangs.

As Queenie walked past them, I noticed she had changed. She now had a wolfish cast to her face, her nose suggesting a bit of a snout. She wore a cape of deerskin. She wore a hood that had stag horns that stood up a foot or two above her head. It seemed more a part of her than something she wore.

Queenie paused at a booth where there stood a tall, gangly troll with a stony beak-like nose. He capered and danced as she looked his way. Among his wares seemed to be a huge fishbowl of blue fireflies the size of hummingbirds. Or maybe they were living balls of blue fire, bouncing off the glass sides of the bowl, and each other. Now she carried Minnie's cage closer, they looked more like tiny winged people, burning blue halos about them and trailing behind as they bounced around.

Judging from the body language of Queenie and the trollish merchant, they were haggling. Queenie pointed back and forth between the bowl and the cage several times. She held up seven fingers, the merchant held up two. Her face clouded and her eyes flashed red. He backed up half a step and held up four fingers. Queenie fixed him with a dangerous stare and picked up the cage, starting to leave.

They settled on five.

Queenie didn't smile until the troll decanted five of the fire creatures into a large jar and handed it to her. He took the cage with Minnie and hung it from a hook over his head. Minnie looked terrified, and her mouth opened in a silent cry.

Queenie's smile became a laugh, and the whole scene dissolved into an orange-red haze. I smelled smoke and felt heat on my legs and one arm. I saw red and white flashing lights mingle with the flickering glow, and heard a siren.

My eyes flew open. The window of the upstairs bedroom I lay in was flashing red and white; the open bedroom door was a rectangle of firelight.

Holy crap!

Although I still felt dizzy from the alcohol, I grabbed up my purse, the poker, and the heavy comforter at the foot of the bed. I slid my feet back into my sandals and put the comforter over me and crawled on the floor toward the door.

The flames were coming from downstairs, and smoke poured up the stairway ceiling. I kept low to the ground, but the further I descended, the worse the heat got. I kept the comforter held between the fire and me and made my careful way to where Stuart lay.

He was gone, and the front door was open. I heard glass break as fire hoses sprayed water into the upstairs windows. The fire billowed onto the ceiling; I had to get out fast.

The dizziness got worse, and I found myself looking up at the ceiling. I'd fallen. I struggled to get to my hands and knees, and when I turned my head, I saw them.

Tiny blue balls of fire darted from couch to chair to desk to curtains, setting things on fire wherever they touched. I could see their gleeful little faces as they darted about the room. One landed on my comforter, and I threw it from me, striking out with the poker. I felt it connect, and one of the little blue things lay still on the ground. Ordinary orange fire spread out in a circle around it.

I rolled, still clutching my purse and poker. I didn't make it to the door before the smoke overcame me and everything went black again.

When I woke, it was to the face of an angel, carrying me away from the burning house. She had a baby face and ancient dark eyes, short brown hair and multiple piercings on either ear. She put me down on the ground, touched my face and shouted over her shoulder. The rosy light of dawn framed my savior.

Someone placed a mask over my mouth and nose, and I breathed in wonderful cool air and felt more alive than I ever had before.

I'd been saved by the smallest firefighter I'd ever seen, but she was strong enough to carry me. She smiled as I tried to sit up. The EMT held me down with a gentle hand and began to examine me.

"What's your name?" I croaked to the angel.

She frowned. "Annabelle, why?"

"I just thought it'd be good to know who saved my life," I replied, and it sounded stupid in my ears.

A warm, bright smile dawned on her lips. "Your boyfriend is okay, he got out and placed the call a few minutes ago. He's scratched up a bit, I'm not sure why, but he'll be fine. You look pretty good to me too, for someone who just got pulled from a fire." She had a boyish voice and stance, but she was beautiful. Everything was beautiful. *I made it out alive!*

Her smile dimmed a few watts. "You should know, hon, he's blaming you for the fire."

I stared at her as though she'd just spoken in a foreign language. When she repeated herself, I looked around for Stuart, but I couldn't see him.

Why would he blame me? I'd done my best to protect him all night!

Damn it, I had to know what was going on!

I brushed off the EMT and rose to my feet.

Stuart sat on the open back of the ambulance, having his blood pressure taken. "Stuart," I said, "There's some kind of misunderstanding, they're saying you blame me for the fire!"

His eyes were cold and hard as they met mine. "Enough is enough, Skye. The firefighters say this spread much too fast to be an accident. I've put up with your drinking and your hallucinations, but you promised me you wouldn't try to kill yourself again. If you were going to break that promise, the least you could do is not take me with you!"

His words hurt so much that I couldn't do anything but run away as fast as I could, bawling all the way.

Chapter Four

I stumbled about halfway to the Monon trail, my eyes too blurry with tears to see. My head pounded from overindulgence last night, and my lungs burned from inhaling smoke. I tripped and landed in a heap on someone's lawn and just lay there sobbing for I don't know how long. I hoped my olive skirt and top would act as camouflage to hide me.

After awhile, there came a feather-light touch of a hand on my shoulder. I stiffened. If it was Stuart, I thought maybe I'd sock him in the face.

I looked up to once again see Annabelle's child-like face framed by the sunrise. She crouched next to me, no longer in her fire-suit, wearing jeans and a long-sleeved white blouse, buttoned all the way up. She looked concerned, but didn't say anything.

"Go 'way," I said between sobs. "I just lost my job, my boyfriend, my home, and a piece of my soul all in one day. I don't care what the EMT needs from me, so unless you're here to arrest me, now's not a good time."

She shook her head. "No, arresting people's not my job. I came because...well, I feel for you, and I had a sort of 'like at first sight'. I think we're kindred spirits, Skye."

My laugh was bitter and nasty. "You? You're little and cute, and you're a hero. I'm a freak. I owe my life to you, but that's not worth a lot right now."

She didn't smile or answer with words. Instead, she withdrew her hand to unbutton her blouse about half-way, holding eye contact with me the whole time. Her face was serious, and my confusion added to my hysterics. I tried to calm myself and wiped at the tears on my face with the back of my hand.

Still without breaking eye contact, Annabelle pulled one side of her blouse aside. She revealed a tattoo of a blackbird coming at me, talons extended, beak open in a savage war cry.

Also, I noticed her shoulder and upper arm had hundreds of very fine white lines in parallel. I recognized with a shock the sight of a cutter's skin. It was such a contrast to her innocent-looking face.

"Freaks know each other on sight, don't you know that?" Her tone was gentle, but there was a rough edge to it that spoke to me of her own pain. "And I saw your wrists, Skye, I've been there too."

Anger fought with the gratitude I'd been feeling for the show of support and caring. "I wasn't trying to kill myself. There's no one that'll believe me about how the fire started."

She bit her lower lip. "I told myself when I came over here that it's not as Firefighter Annabelle, but as just Annabelle. But I can't help but ask. If you want to tell me, I'll believe you."

The anger kept my rant going. I sat up now, to see more eye to eye. "Fine, you asked for it. An evil fairy queen sent blue fire sprites after Stuart, or maybe me, to burn our place down and kill us. Believe me?"

Annabelle studied me and nodded. "I saw something when I was in there. Blue balls of flame, darting around. All I could think was you had some kind of gas leak or that bottles of high-proof liquor were exploding. Either might make blue fire. But I thought the flames looked alive. It seemed crazy to think that."

My rage at the world was extinguished as though she'd thrown a bucket of water at me. "You...you saw them too? It's totally crazy, I know. But that's my world. I see things like that all the time. M-mostly when I drink. It's easier that way, they're more solid."

She blinked. "Why do you have to drink to see them? You're sure...well, I don't mean to be a jerk, but you're sure it's not just the alcohol making you hallucinate?"

I nodded. "I'm sure. I've never been more sure than now. I dreamed about the blue fire sprites and woke up to see them setting fire to my house."

She thought for a moment. "And your soul, what did you mean by that? Your boyfriend might reconsider after he calms down and gets a fat insurance check. And even if he doesn't, losing a guy isn't the end of the world; your soul is still all yours. He gives up his claim on his piece if he dumps you, you know?"

I laughed. "No, you're misunderstanding. I wasn't being figurative about losing part of my soul. There's a bit of me that got lost a couple of years ago, it's hard to explain. But it...she...took on a life of her own, and she was kidnapped while I slept. I dreamed what she saw."

I was losing Annabelle with this fantastic talk. She'd crossed her arms, though her blouse was still unbuttoned to the bottom of her sternum. *She must think I'm a liar or a nutcase.*

"Skye, I'm trying to believe you, I am," she said, "Freaks need to stick together, so if you need me to believe you, I will, but it's not something I've experienced the way you do. I've never met anyone like you. Is there anything I can do to help?"

I thought about this a moment. I decided to be daring. I was out of things to risk, aside from my purse and its contents, plus one iron poker. She'd taken a risk showing me herself, and maybe she was even risking her job by leaving the scene of the fire to go after me.

What the hell.

"Yeah, you can. Can you give me a ride somewhere?"

She glanced over her shoulder, then back at me. "I can give you a ride back to the station, but my shift is another couple of hours. I've been up all night, but this is the only call I've been on."

I shook my head. "I can't go back there, I can't be around Stuart right now. I lost my job going after him, and he blames me even though I stayed up most of the night guarding him."

She looked torn, looking back at the flashing fire trucks, then at me again.

I didn't want to start off a new friendship by asking her to sacrifice her job.

"Tell you what. I'll catch a bus downtown. If you really want to help, can you meet me at Holliday Park after you get off?"

I watched her eyes. They went from furrowed and worried to clear and calm. She smiled. "Yeah, I can do that."

"Bring silver and cold iron if you can," I added. "We might have to fight for my soul."

She laughed, but cut it short when she saw I wasn't laughing with her. "Seriously? Rock on. I'm up for an adventure. But right now, I gotta go, and you gotta make yourself seriously scarce, unless you want to spend the day being questioned. It's too bad I couldn't find you, you know?"

I gave her a sudden, impulsive hug. I whispered my thanks in her ear. She returned the hug with a fierceness I didn't expect. She pulled away just far enough to look in my eyes, then she brushed my lips with hers.

Then she broke the contact and waved her farewell and turned to march back toward the fire scene. I watched her go for a few seconds, touching my fingers to my lips. I'd never been kissed by a girl who wasn't a relative before. *Huh.*

I did have an urgent need to not be there, however. I took her advice and made my way toward the Monon, with more care and stealth this time. At least if I was followed by anyone else, they'd have to make it on foot.

No one did follow me, to my relief. I felt the cool morning air on my face and loved the way it made my skirt billow out behind me as I walked. It felt cleansing after the night of booze, fear and fire.

I reached Leslie's place, hoping for a shoulder to cry on, maybe a ride, and with luck, a change of clothes. He wasn't home. I thought about calling him, but this was his work shift, and I didn't want to get him into trouble.

Hmm. I had someplace I needed to go, and as much as I wanted a change of clothes and a shower, I'd have to get there as-is, for now. I walked another couple of blocks to a bus stop and waited. I rummaged in my purse and found my 31 day pass, and waited a few minutes to catch the downtown bus.

I boarded and found that the bus was already crowded. The driver eyed the poker in my hand, but I pretended to need it as a walking stick, and he rolled his eyes and waved me on. I thought I'd have to stand, but a twitchy guy with his pants belted around his thighs showed his chivalrous side and offered his seat to me. I wedged myself between a mousy professional lady and dozing old man in sweatpants. We made two stops before the folks on either side of me mumbled excuses and stood up further back in the bus.

Huh. I guess I smelled like campfire. Very much so. I wouldn't have guessed that I'd ever end up as the stereotypical stinky person on the bus. I felt embarrassed, since even people two seats away from me were giving me looks, working at the latches on the windows to crack them open.

We passed 38th street, about halfway downtown now, when a tiny man sat next to me. I thought at first he had dwarfism, but then the sun flashed on him through a gap in buildings and trees, and I caught a violet aura shining around him, just for an instant. He wriggled to push his butt far back into the seat. I looked away, not wanting more otherworldly entanglements. I also didn't want to drink anymore, not until I had to. My fingers tightened around the handle of the poker.

His hot little hand slid down my forearm and clasped my other hand in his, lacing his fingers with mine. His palms were damp with sweat. I turned, intending on pulling back my hand to slap him, but his dazzling smile made my mind go all foggy.

"Well, lass, it seems yer in a pickle, and that's a fact, innit?" It surprised me how deep his voice sounded. He appeared to be scruffy but kindly. His clothes hung loose on him, and the colors clashed. His greasy hair was held in place by a crown made of aluminum foil. Jolly rancher hard candies stuck to this makeshift band like sticky rectangular gems. They caught the morning sunlight with a surprising beauty.

My brain wouldn't form coherent words, so my nasty retort softened to a dull "uh huh."

His smile dimmed and he leaned in. We were old chums, sharing a laugh. "You going up against her, are ye? Queen Bitch, I mean, her what steals yer soul and makes ya dance like a marionette?"

I nodded, some of my anger returning enough to burn off a bit of the fog. "You bet I am. I don't know what she's got in for me, but I'm not playing her game by her rules."

He squeezed my hand and whacked his knee with his free one. "There's the spirit, eh? But ye'll need some help, some friends, I'll say. She's a nasty piece of work and that's for sure."

I glanced down at our interlaced fingers and he shrugged and let my hand go. And winked at me.

"Friends are always welcome," I said with caution. "Who are you?"

With a courtly flourish, he bowed there in his seat, looking a bit comical. "Ah forgive me, lass, but I had to see that I had the right one before introducing myself." I noticed that the sounds of people, and even the engines and bumping of the road, now quieted and moved far away. It was as though we had privacy in this very public bus.

"I'm the Transit King," he said. "At your service, lass."

I laughed. I couldn't stop myself. I'd told crazier things to a stranger only half an hour ago but this was beyond even my capacity for suspension of belief. "You're what?"

His smile remained, and he patted my knee like I was his favorite niece. "Eh, I suppose ye don't see me as I am, the glamour is too strong for even the likes of you to pierce. I thought ye had the Sight. That's the word on the lines, anyway. I rule the straight tracks, at least the ones that move. Nothing that happens in my domain goes without my notice. I wanted to offer some assistance."

Transit King? Now I'd heard everything. Was there a Duke of the Sewers, maybe? A Prince of the Parks? Maybe the Transit King waged eternal war against the Parking Gods. *Too much!*

So I bluffed. "What kind of help?"

The Transit King brightened. "Well, for starters, in return for some information now and again, I'll grant ye asylum while you travel on me buses."

I wondered if IndyGo knew about this.

I nodded. "That's kind of you."

"And in exchange for a favor promised, I'll give ye a bit o' magic." He produced a coin, which he pressed into my hand.

I looked at it. In my palm sat a corroded brass coin, its faces weathered almost smooth, except for the word "interurban" curving along the edge on one side.

"It's a rail token from some of me better days," he said with sadness, "Hold it and say "pick me up" thrice, and no matter where you be, a ride will come to yer rescue, ta take you anywhere within my domain ye need to go."

I looked at him, then back at the coin, doubtful.

He sighed. "Yeah, thought so. I'll bet ye got no one else who believes you've got the Sight, eh?"

"Not many," I admitted.

"Belief takes faith, dearie, and not just in yourself. Extend me this belief and you'll take a step toward being believed yerself, mark my words!" He looked out the window, "I think this is yer stop, hmm?"

The little man was right. I pulled the cable and slipped the coin into my bra. *Who knows, if it does what he says, maybe I'll need it.*

He smiled, watching the coin disappear with a playful leer. "Keepin' the coin does obligate ye to one favor after ye use it. Anything I ask."

Anything?

The bus was slowing to a stop.

"But..." I objected, standing.

"Don't worry yer pretty head, I won't ask much, certainly not to compromise yer honor. But what kind o' King would I be if I gave it all away for free?"

I didn't have time to answer this. The driver honked his horn in impatience and I had to rush to get off before the doors closed.

As the bus rolled away, I caught sight of the little King in the windows, and a reflection superimposed a different image over his face, just for an instant. In that flash, I saw an older, scarred face, but with flowing dark hair and a silver crown with real gems set in it. His parting wink made me laugh for no reason I could explain.

So, first things first. I walked a couple of blocks off the bus route to the Super SaveInn. A room would be a terrible extravagance while out of work, but I didn't want to sleep under a bridge or make a hasty decision as to whose couch I'd sleep on until I got back on my feet. I had enough for a few days in my debit account, and Starbucks owed me a week's pay.

I had to push aside panic. Worrying about being jobless and homeless wouldn't get me anywhere, and I had more important things to take care of before I could worry much about those problems.

Like taking a shower.

The guy at the hotel front desk was about my age, kinda cute, but he had a stick up his ass. He asked for three forms of ID and scrutinized these like I was applying for a passport. He ran my card, and it came up good, which helped. After he was satisfied, he spent an awful long time typing away at his terminal before swiping a card-key for me, offered in a paper envelope covered with pictures of the hotel restaurant and Domino's Pizza logos.

"So, hot stuff," I asked, just to get a rise out of him, "Is there a gift shop in this place?"

He allowed himself a careful, rationed smile and lowered his eyes as he nodded. "Down the hall, past the elevators, near the pool."

Good. Even reeking of house fire, hung over, with serious bed-head, I could still make a guy blush. Nice to know I hadn't lost *everything.*

The gift shop had essentials, and I picked up more or less one of everything. In addition to toiletries, I grabbed a couple of touristy t-shirts. I also picked up a novelty sardine tin that claimed to contain an emergency pair of panties, a pad and a condom. I needed the first a lot more than the others.

Beggars can't be choosers.

It all rang up to an amount that made me wince, but my haste made thriftiness impractical just now.

I rode the elevator up to my floor with my new purchases. *Wow, I just doubled my total worldly goods,* I thought. Right away, I regretted that bit of gallows humor, as my mood sank back into gloom and doom.

Once in my room, I set about fixing that. I set my purse, gift shop bag, and the magic token on the bed closest to the bathroom. I leaned the fireplace poker on the nightstand. I stripped and filled the sink with hot soapy water, trying not to flash back to the previous night of tending to...

Stop it!

Anyway, I washed my smoky clothing, including the only bra I owned now, there in the sink. I wrung everything out, rinsed, and hung things up on hooks and chairs around the room.

Then I took a shower myself. *Oh, hot water never felt so damned good.* The smoke and stress sloughed off of me and swirled down the drain. I shampooed my hair twice and just stood under the massaging spray and cried again, letting it all out where no one could see or hear.

Then I thought of the kiss Annabelle the firefighter gave me. I still wasn't sure how to feel about that. I felt warm gratitude to my new friend for showing me compassion and relating to me like we'd known each other for years. There, alone in the shower, I had to admit the kiss was a nice touch, whether it was just friendly or meant something more.

More important, she was willing to help out, and didn't run away when I told her my secrets.

Assuming she showed up later.

Stop it...

That reminded me, I only had another hour to get dressed and take a bus up to Holliday Park as promised. I sighed and got out of the shower.

And in the mirror, I saw a gargoyle out in the main room. It had improbable large tusks, deep sunken eyes, a hunched back and clawed hands and feet. It toyed with a coin, holding it up to the light. *The Transit King's token.*

I whirled and didn't see anything except the coin floating in mid-air. "Hey! That's mine! The Transit King gave it to me! You are not welcome in my home!"

One thing I've learned about the people of the shadow world was that the fairy legends had it right. They could be tricky and nasty, but they all played by rules. Those rules were pretty firm on ownership. Plus, invoking the name of someone powerful never hurt.

The coin dropped to the floor. I grabbed at a towel to cover myself with and glanced in the mirror on the door to one side of the room. The gargoyle cowered in a corner. I wrapped the towel around me and grabbed the iron poker and walked to the door, holding it open.

"Get out!" I said with as much authority as I could while dripping wet.

I didn't see or hear him pass, but I felt a *whuff* of air as he slipped past me and out into the hall.

A surprised housekeeper stared at me. "Something is wrong?"

I didn't know what to say, so I just shook my head and shut the door and slid the bolt shut. I shook just a little as I crossed the room and picked up my token. Adrenaline surged through me. I was shaken by the invasion of my room, but felt the power of having intimidated a boogieman.

"Go Team Skye!" I cheered to the empty room, laughing with relief.

I cracked open the sardine tin and pulled out wrinkled pink panties that had the nerve to say "oops!" all over them. Whoever thought that joke up should be shot.

I put them on anyway, though they fit a bit too loose on my caboose. My bra was still very damp, so I spent too much time using the hair dryer on it. When it was dry enough, I put it on. *Mmmm, toasty boobies.* I slipped on my denim mini-skirt from my purse and decided on an Indianapolis Indians t-shirt. That fit well at any rate. I wished for my boots, but in this heat, my thick sandals would be a better choice anyway. I slipped the token back in my bra for safekeeping.

All clean, I was reluctant to pick up my purse, since it still smelled of the fire. I went to the door and found the maid a few doors down. She turned out to be willing to loan me some deodorizing spray, which helped more than I thought it would. I sprayed my drip-drying clothes too, just for good measure.

I put on my rings and reached in my purse to get out my pendant with the chip in it. *No. Too soon.* I put it back for now.

I grabbed up the poker, wishing it was something small enough to put in my purse, or somehow less conspicuous.

I left the hotel and found my timing was just right, I got on the bus that'd take me past the park just before that one departed. This driver was too jaded to even look at my poker. I said a cheery hello and swiped my card and found a seat to myself. The outbound bus was just about empty this time of the morning.

Almost. A skater girl moved up from the back to the seat across the aisle from me. I thought maybe she should be in school, but remembered that school would be out of session in late June. She stared at me awhile, then said, "Hey. Sofia. You're Baroness Sofia, ain't ya?"

I'm always surprised when I'm recognized outside of the game. I try hard to look mysterious and exotic and *different* than Everyday Skye. I *feel* like a different person when I play the powerful vampiress. I studied the girl and thought she looked familiar as well, but wasn't sure.

"Yes?" I didn't want to invite more conversation than necessary.

"Ha! I knew it. Good one last week, tripping Her Queenliness. Someone needs to put her in her place, she's too new to be so high and mighty." The girl's grin was wicked and gleeful.

Huh? Last week... last week...

Oh!

Now I remembered. In-game, I'd asked for an audience with the Night Duke, ruler of the local club. Queenie had too. Time ran short, and she got bumped because I had seniority, as the Duke decided it. She had to wait until the Danse to get his ear, and he'd be preoccupied with all sorts of politics and partying.

Maybe that's what pissed her off? *If so, wow, thin skin much?*

I played it cool. I waved off the congratulations. "I really wasn't trying, I just needed to settle some business. The Duke's the one who made the decision, I didn't twist his arm."

The kid shrugged and seemed a little disappointed. She put on her headphones and listened to music the rest of the trip.

We bounced along the road and stopped only a few times along the way to let people on and off. When we reached the twisty, hilly Spring Mill Road, I got ready and pulled the cord as the park appeared.

As I got off the bus, the kid made a little gun with her finger and grinned as she mouthed "bang bang" as some sort of farewell. I shot back with my left hand.

Strange.

I'd forgotten just how big Holliday Park was. I hadn't specified just where to meet, so I walked around the paved edge the long way, paths into the woods beckoning me as I passed. The fabulous but fake ruins loomed up in the middle of the path. I failed to see my new friend in the playground and picnic areas or the parking lots.

What if she doesn't come? I don't want to do this alone.

I debated a second circuit of the park when an old SUV pulled into the lot where I stood. Annabelle hopped out and bounded toward me. I met her with a hug. She still smelled like my burning apartment house, but I didn't mind so much.

When we each took a step back, she looked me over. "Hey, you clean up nice!"

I felt color warm my cheeks, standing there in the sun with her. "I... I was afraid you wouldn't show up."

She made a rude noise with her tongue. "And turn down an adventure? No way."

"So you're saying you believe me?"

She nodded. "I wasn't sure this morning, but I am now."

"Huh?"

She pointed at the pavement.

I looked around, but wasn't sure what she meant. I stared at her, confused. "I don't see anything, Annabelle."

"Exactly! I don't either!"

"Okay, excuse my witty banter, but... huh?"

She pointed again. "I cast a shadow. You don't. Now let's go find that bit of your soul, 'k?"

Chapter Five

I gaped at my lack of shadow. I think it surprised me more than Annabelle. You'd think Minnie's past antics animating it would make its loss less of a shock. I bent down and waved my hand over the ground, fascinated. I held the same hand up between my eyes and the sun, and it still blocked the light to my eyes.

This proved that all this, all along, existed more than just inside my own head. I fought back tears and threw my arms around Annabelle and laughed.

"Come on, what are you doing? Let's go!" Annabelle's voice contained more excitement than impatience.

"Okay, okay!" I said, taking a step back to grin at her. Then, I rummaged around in my purse and came up with the bottle of vodka I'd stowed there last night. I uncapped it, took a couple of breaths, then gulped down a big mouthful of the rather tasteless alcohol. Fire traced down my esophagus and ignited my stomach.

"Hey, hey! Slow down there!" Annabelle sounded alarmed.

"Told you," I gasped, "I can only see fairies if I'm sloshed. Well, at least a little tipsy."

"So, we came here so you could drink? And what next? Why Holliday Park?"

I held up a finger and took another gulp before capping the bottle. "Whew! Well, the piece of my soul is a little person, I call her Minnie. Yeah, I know, silly, hmm?"

Annabelle gave me a crooked grin and waited for me to go on.

"Anyway, Minnie was kidnapped on the Monon last night. By a bitch that calls herself Queenie in the Vampire game."

Annabelle held up a hand to stop me. "Whoa there. Game? No way you're telling me all of this is some kind of game."

I shook my head. "No, not this, not here and now. I'm just part of a live action role-playing game that involves a vampire court. So's Stuart. But along comes Queenie and her eggplants, and in a short time, she's taken over the game. Or just about. Anyway. She looks like a sweet young thing, but I'm sure there's a lot more to her than even I'm seeing. Queen Bitch took Minnie away in a cage to this park, into the woods, where there's a circle of stones on top of a hill. She used that circle to go to...I don't know, Fairyland...some other place I've never seen before. I saw how she did it, and I recognized that circle of stones, since this is one of my favorite places. It's in the woods a ways, where a few paths come together."

"Ohhh...I see. And so you'll be seeing things that I can't see?"

I nodded.

"So I'll be basically blind?"

I hadn't thought of it that way. "I guess so..."

"Gimmie," she said, and she grabbed the bottle of vodka from me. I worried she was trying to keep me from drinking any more, but she took a swig of the clear alcohol, too.

"Uh, that's not going to help you see anything," I said.

"Yeah, I didn't think so, but a little liquid courage can't be all bad," she said, and handed the bottle back with a wink.

I laughed, but didn't feel it. If someone who ran into burning buildings to save people like me was scared, what did I think I was doing?

I put the booze away and took her hand to lead her out of the parking lot and onto the paved walkway that led to the trails. We were passed a few times by joggers and rollerbladers. I told myself that holding her hand was to comfort her, but just now, it meant a lot to me to have her here, believing me and helping me.

At the head of the trail, the woods of Holliday Park loomed darker and denser than I remembered. We exchanged glances. Annabelle stuck her tongue out at me, crossed her eyes, and screwed up her face.

I laughed, and the laughter dissolved into an unstoppable giggling fit. Which made her laugh, and that became the funniest thing in the world to me. Was it the booze, or was it nerves? I did feel a little dizzy...

Then something stopped me, cold.

I'd caught a glimpse of something I'd never seen in the park before. In the place of the artsy false ruins stood a mighty castle, not at all ruined. Its walls were made of cemented fieldstones, and it rose at least a couple of stories above the park.

It even had a moat for God's sake.

Annabelle stopped her giggling and followed my stare and said, "What? What do you see?"

"Uh," I said.

"What? What? You tell me, you hear? I'm blind, Skye, help me out," she pleaded, tugging at my sleeve.

Oh. Oops. I thought of those damned silly panties from the tin that I had on. I let out a groan at the thought.

"Damn it!" she play-smacked me on the shoulder, though maybe a bit harder than I was used to playing.

"Ow! Sorry! There's a friggin' castle, right there where the ruins should be!"

"You're kidding," she said, eyes dancing as she tried to read my expression to tell if I was pulling her leg.

"No, seriously. Never saw that before. Never been this tipsy here before, either."

"Huh. Maybe this is obvious, but I don't see anything," she said, looking back over at where I'd been staring.

I shrugged. "I didn't see it there earlier when I walked around the park, either." I tore my gaze from the structure and back to the dark of the woods. "Anyway, let's get going. The portal is in the woods, not the castle."

The trail started as a switchback down a steep grade, some stone steps set into the hill here and there to help ease our descent. We couldn't go hand-in-hand without tripping on each other, which made me sad.

The trail became much less steep as it followed the side of a ridge along a ravine. I could see other hikers on the opposite side, making their way up. I glanced back behind us. No one was following us. No things, either. The entrance disappeared from view. Though the sun pierced the canopy of leaves here and there, the gloom closed in on us more than it ought to have on one of the longest days of the year.

That thought led me to thinking about the Danse Macabre. This year's theme was Midsummer, since it was being held so close to the Solstice. As I thought about it more, it seemed like a bad night for vampires, since it'd be one of the shortest. Maybe vamps celebrated the return of longer nights on Midsummer the way we celebrate the return of longer days in the middle of winter?

Annabelle plodded along the path, a big smile on her face, despite the gloom. Funny how she led the way, even though I was the one who knew how to get to the circle of stones. She was sweet, being protective of me. I bet she didn't even realize she was doing it.

I decided that Annabelle was a 'keeper' as friends go. I've heard of love at first sight, but best friends at first sight? Well, why not? Friendship is a beautiful form of love. It's sometimes more enduring than romantic love, I thought. Stuart's face appeared in my mind's eye.

Stop it!

At the bottom of the ravine, we came to a fork in the road. Annabelle stopped, turned, and looked to me for guidance. I started to go left, but felt a sudden chill from that direction.

Frogs croaked a deep song, first disorganized, then more and more in unison and with greater and greater power. I heard gravel crunch under many heavy feet.

Annabelle started to ask, "What?" but I covered her mouth for a moment to hush her. I dragged her along the trail by the hand in the wrong direction.

We sped along as quiet as we could, still holding onto each other. We crossed a small wooden bridge and climbed up onto a raised area surrounding a stagnant pond. Oily water slopped over a ledge in a narrow opening to babble under the bridge we'd crossed. We slipped past stone and wood park benches up here, for those who just couldn't get eaten alive by enough mosquitoes elsewhere in the park. I led her down and off the path to one side, away from the pool, and pulled her down to hunker with me in the tall weeds.

I held my finger to my lips and jerked my head to point back the way we'd come. As Annabelle's eyes darted back and forth, a wild, hunted look haunted them.

The rotting smell of the pond was overwhelmed by a putrid odor that washed over us. I wondered if Annabelle could smell it. I wanted to throw up, but held it down like my life depended on it. It just might.

The marching steps came closer, and a troupe of frogmen crossed the bridge. They walked on two legs, though they hunched over and bobbed their improbably wide heads in time with their steps. They looked more like Murlocs from World of Warcraft than they looked like the Swamp Thing.

Also, they wore uniforms of purple with gold sashes. They carried what I thought were tall walking sticks, but as they got closer, I could see the glint of sharp metal points.

They stopped, and several of them started sniffing and snuffling around. How they could smell anything over themselves baffled me.

"Oy! I fink I found somefing!" called the one nearest to us.

"Wot? I don't smell nuffing," said another, nearby.

"Thats' 'cause you've had more than a snootful yerself. Her ladyship said we're on guard for a chickie what smells like a fireplace and mebbe like she's had somefing strong. That's wot I smells! Off here, off the trail."

Crap. Maybe deodorizer fooled my nose, but my purse and Annabelle still smelled like smoke, and both of us had been drinking vodka.

The frogmen pushed and shoved to get a better whiff, and panic rose up in me. I got the impression Annabelle felt the same. I pointed back the way we'd come, squeezed her hand and whispered as quiet as I could in her ear, "On my signal, run back that way!"

She nodded, and took a deep breath. There's no way she could smell the frogmen or she couldn't do that without gagging.

I waited as the frogmen left the trail. I reached into my purse and pulled out a small tube.

I waited as they crept closer, snuffling and sniffing. Even Annabelle twitched as one of them snapped a twig underfoot.

I held up the tube in front of me and aimed. I waited until I could feel their nauseous breath on my skin.

Then I let them have it. Pepper spray's pretty nasty on a human's mucous membranes, but these guys? They seemed to be made of nothing but mucous membranes.

The frogmen screamed and fell backwards. I yanked on Annabelle's arm, and we took off running.

The underbrush tore at our clothes and skin, the muddy ground under our feet threatened to send us sprawling, but we didn't look back. I could hear the frogmen's piteous yowls, but I could also hear one set of feet pounding after us. We leaped over the trickling stream instead of crossing the bridge. Annabelle almost fell, but I was right behind her, and my momentum pushed her forward, so she didn't end up going back into the slimy water.

We pelted our way up the path away from the pool, past the trail marker where we'd come down from the main park. Still the flapping, running steps followed behind us. The steps were very close now. I heard slurping, croaking, and panting.

I shouted, "Keep going, I'll catch up!" and whirled around and whipped my iron poker through the air behind me without even looking.

I was lucky. He'd been right on my heels, and the poker caught him right across the face. I didn't feel a strong impact, but where it struck him, it was as though the iron was right from a blacksmith's fire, his froggy flesh seared and bubbled in a long line.

He hissed and backpedaled. I menaced him with the poker, making another, thinner line of seared skin across his enormous bulbous throat.

He fell to the ground, covering his head with webbed hands and dropped his pike. He groveled and wept, and I relented.

I turned to run after Annabelle. She was still standing there on the path, watching me with eyes almost as bugged out as the froggies.

"Damn it, I told you to keep running!" I said, catching my breath.

"I couldn't leave you!"

"Yes, you could. You're blind, remember?"

"Well, how do I know where we're going?"

"Doesn't matter!" I cried, "We're being chased. GO!"

She started to reply, but I'd already started running, gravel from the trail slipping from under my feet as I went. Not to be left behind, Annabelle caught up with me.

"What..." she panted, "what was back there, Skye?"

"Frogs," I replied, more out of breath than she was. "Big 'uns. Sharp sticks. Pointy."

She dared a quick look back over her shoulder, shook her head and kept running with me.

The path had a slight incline upwards, and soon we reached another intersection. The stones had numbers etched into them. I motioned for Annabelle to follow me up the steeper one, marked with a number 6 and many arrows indicating a longer path.

Out of necessity, we slowed down about halfway up. Annabelle looked around her, eyes still wild and fearful. I put a hand on her arm and murmured, "I think we lost them, for the moment," but didn't feel as sure about that statement as I sounded. Once they recovered from the pepper spray, they'd find us with those bloodhound noses of theirs.

I'd have to worry about that later.

I snuck out my vodka bottle and supplemented the tingliness throughout my body and the buzzing in my head with another swallow.

Annabelle gave me a worried look, but when I offered her the bottle, she didn't refuse it. She closed her eyes and handed the vodka back to me, calming herself by force of will.

After a minute or three, we stopped shaking and got our breathing slower toward normal. I led her up the steeper hill step by step, walking rather than running now.

Just as in the dream, several paths converged at the top of the hill, each marked with a stone, and inside that ring of stones was a smaller ring of stones, each big enough to sit on as a lumpy natural seat.

And just as in the dream, it seemed like night here, the sunlight no longer filtered through the branches, having been replaced by the moon.

I checked the clock on my cell phone, and it disagreed with what I saw around me, its time showing just before noon in the a.m.

"So, what do you see?" I asked Annabelle.

"I see a circle of stones, just like you said."

"No, I mean, is there anything strange about this place?"

She considered, looking around, shading her eyes as she looked up. "Not really. It's pretty damn quiet. I don't hear birds or other animals here."

Hmm, I hadn't noticed that before. "To me, it looks like night."

"Nope," she said, "still daytime for me."

Night and day. It shouldn't surprise me, but my long habit of keeping my visions to myself kept me from asking questions about what others saw when I knew my second sight had kicked in.

Annabelle shifted from foot to foot, glancing back down the trail we'd come from. "Okay Skye, we're here. What are you gonna do, cast a summoning spell or something to bring back your soul-bit?"

Well, crap. I hadn't thought this far ahead. "Well, I don't know any spells, I'm not Wiccan like my friend Babette."

"How'd Queenie do it?"

I pointed to the center of the ring of stones, and Annabelle walked over there, folding her hands in front of her, waiting.

"Well, I saw Queenie do this, but didn't hear what she was saying. Here goes nothing!"

I started to walk around the circle clockwise, as I'd seen the fairy woman do. After several trips around, I felt some kind of static electricity build up on my skin, and my clothing and hair billowed out like I was Bill Nye the Science Guy holding onto a Van de Graaf generator.

"Is it working?" Annabelle asked. "'Cause I'm getting dizzy watching you go round and round..."

I shook my head, not sure if I should speak. I kept getting hazy glimpses of a white tunnel ahead of me, but only if I looked to one side and caught it in my peripheral vision. Walking around the stones took effort, like walking into a strong headwind.

After five minutes of that, I stopped, tired, frustrated and more than a little dizzy from walking in circles while tipsy. Annabelle jerked her head around to look down the path we'd come up. I listened.

I could hear froggy voices shouting off in the distance, coming closer.

Damn.

Think, Skye, think! Well, if I'd pushed it this far, maybe I needed more of the same. I drank down at least as much vodka as I'd already had. I felt it add to the world's tilted spinning around me. I wobbled a bit as I put the bottle back.

"Here, hold this," I said, handing the iron poker to Annabelle. Maybe it was interfering with the magic of the place? She accepted it, facing trail 6, looking ready to lash out with the heavy iron improvised weapon at any moment.

I started again. I stumbled. I felt a little sick. Then I thought of Minnie, trapped in the iron cage, up for sale in the market I'd seen. I pictured the underground world that housed the market. I could see the bobbing colorful lights from my dream if I tried.

"Skye..." came Annabelle's warning. I could hear it too, frogmen feet flapping up the hill. All noise from the hill came as from a distance, my ears overwhelmed by a roaring as the static electricity became visible, crackling from my fingers and feet. The tunnel came up again, and I approached a more solid entrance, like a luminous cave. It whirled and spun around like something out of a fun house, or maybe Doctor Who.

The resistance had grown as I walked, feeling as though I waded waist-deep in a pool, down toward the deep end. I knew that I would not be able to turn back after the next few steps.

I heard the cries of the frogmen foot soldiers, but couldn't see them through the walls of white that surrounded the circle, Annabelle, and me.

No turning back, I decided, and stepped over the threshold.

Annabelle gasped. "I see something, Skye! I really see it!"

I sure hoped she meant the white walls of energy that I'd built as I walked along, and not our pursuers. I didn't dare speak for fear of losing my concentration.

The tunnel became more defined and straightened out. I didn't feel like I was walking in a circle anymore, but I still saw Annabelle rotating off to my right as she had before. The resistance slowed my progress quite a bit now, and I had the sensation of being on fire, but without heat or pain. I fought the dizziness that grew with each step as the liquor spread through me. I became terrified of stumbling. I didn't know where Annabelle and I would end up if I fell before I got to the end of the tunnel. Would we reappear upon the hill to be skewered by frogs, would we emerge in the caves of the market, or would we be lost in some *otherspace* in-between?

I shivered. I knew I didn't have the answers. I knew that playing with fire paled in comparison with messing with magics I didn't understand. What if we were lost, even now?

My breath wasn't coming easy now, the air had become thin and icy cold, and my lungs ached with each gasp. I focused on the image of my Minnie in my head. She's a part of me, I thought, even if we're separated. We want to be together, we can't help it. This path must lead to her. I imagined I could feel the pull of my tiny other self and pushed on in that direction with all my might. The roar of the wind and sparks filled my ears. I had to put a hand up to shade my eyes from the painful glare of the vortex of white light. I began to notice a dark center ahead, a hole that opened wider with each step.

I hoped that was the dark at the end of the tunnel.

I could only just make out Annabelle, who now sat in what had been the circle, arms hugging her knees to her chest, face hidden entirely. For just a moment, my thoughts strayed from Minnie to Annabelle, out of concern.

That's when I stumbled and fell, knocked backwards by the force of the vortex. I cried out, but landed on my back hard enough to knock the air from my lungs. I became disoriented as shreds of the tunnel of energy flew apart in tatters. Terror took over and drunken animal panic blotted out any useful thoughts. I struggled for breath and flailed around me with my arms and legs as though drowning.

I kicked something hard that didn't budge, smashing several toes against a rough surface. I failed to scream and found a new tunnel as my vision began to close in, a blacker darkness enveloping the nowhere sky and fainter crackling arcs of electricity around me.

One of my hands smacked into something warm and firm. The something grabbed my wrist with a strong grip. In my panicked state, I went wild, trying to tear my arm free. After an eternity, I could draw a ragged breath. I bashed my free fist into the something that held onto me a couple of times.

The something didn't let go of my wrist as it landed on top of me, and I found my other wrist grabbed and pinned to the ground. I screamed and thrashed and felt sure I was going to vomit.

Then I heard a voice. It was calling a name. My name. Screaming my name. Cursing at me.

A face or two was bobbing around in front of me. It was the source of the screaming. The face or faces came into focus as my panic receded just a little. Annabelle. Annabelle was the something that had me pinned down. Shouldn't she be somewhere else?

"Skye, you drunk-ass bitch, wake up! I think the whole damned world is falling apart around us and I can't do what you do. I need you!"

I finally stopped my fighting and went slack under her. She still kept me pinned down, panting with the effort of our struggles.

"Nghugh," I grunted, ever full of sparkling conversation. I cleared my throat and took a breath, "I screwed up, I tripped, we're lost," I wailed.

She sat up, releasing my wrists, though she still straddled my legs. Her chestnut hair fell from behind one ear to obscure one of her eyes as she looked down at me. "I'm sorry, there's no time to feel sorry for yourself, hon. You got us here, you can get us further.

Just where 'here' might be was as complete a mystery as I'd ever known. I tried to sit up, and she got off my lap so I could look around. There was a sooty black mist or smoke billowing around this place, sparks arcing between one cloud and another much less often now, the brilliant light and tunnel had flown apart and blown away.

I saw no sign of the hole or the path of the tunnel that marked what I thought was our way out.

However, I did see movement among the black mist. Blobs of elastic smoky material stretched towards us. The inky pseudopods developed features, shiny black marbles for eyes, and splits in the ends yawned open into mouths, opening wider and wider. We shrank back from the longest of these, but before they reached us, the mouths opened wide enough to turn the creatures inside out, rolling back into the mist surrounding us.

I heard a delayed scream that sounded as fake as a B movie heroine's, but realized it was me when Annabelle whirled to stare at me. "There are monsters in the mist," I said.

She nodded. "I know. I can see now that I'm here."

Come to think of it, I wasn't sure how we could see anything at all. If I had to guess, I'd say in this place, Annabelle and I gave off our own light, and all else was darkness.

The mouths kept stretching toward us, then melted back. We stayed in the center of the stones, which seemed to be a natural border that the mist and the creatures didn't like to cross. I began to hear a whispering, though at first, not specific words, but gibberish, not like any language I'd seen. If anything, it was too repetitive in rhythm. I caught snatches of the same sort-of phrases that came around like....

Like singing. Toneless, wordless singing. I decided to sing the first thing that came to mind to see what happened.

"Show me the way to go home, I'm tired and I wanna go to bed...."

Annabelle shot me a strange look, but she joined in after the point when the words reverse.

"Home me the way to go show, I'm bed and I wanna go to tired...."

The effect was disturbing. Ever seen a snake charmer? Imagine dozens of black blobby snakes snapping and popping and twining their necks, melting together and dissolving.

Yeah okay, I didn't say it'd be easy to picture.

Annabelle and I stood up to sing louder as we started the silly song over again. It was just the kind of goofy thing Minnie would do. Now that I thought about it, the last time I had woken up with a hangover, still drunk, Minnie'd tortured me by singing choruses of this song and "Henry the 8th" until I begged her, sobbing that she had to stop. She'd laughed and disappeared.

Minnie danced now in my mind's eye, and I could feel the direction I had to go. I took a step toward the boiling mass of black mist and mouthing blobs. Annabelle grabbed my arm to stop me, but I shrugged her off and took another step. The mist and the monsters retreated as I advanced; they parted to let me out of the circle. Annabelle followed me, and if she could get any closer to me, I thought she'd climb right up my back.

We sang that old drinking song over and over, six or seven times through, when we reached the other side, and a straight path stretched out into the dark ahead of us. I imagined I heard a "snap" as the cloud closed behind us.

Sparks rose around us, and this time, I kept my mind on Minnie, letting Annabelle follow as near as she could. No vortex this time rose around us, and no black hole opened, but the dark began to crowd around, our steps echoing off some roof and walls that arched over us unseen.

The arch over us narrowed to a cave, and we had to bend our heads to keep from scraping the stone above us. Then we had to hunch, bend almost double, and at last we were forced to crawl.

Then the cave opened up into a vast underground area. The underground market stretched before us, merry lights of all colors pushing back the gloom ahead.

Chapter Six

When we arrived, Annabelle and I clung to each other in relief, sitting on the damp cave floor. The air was chilly enough that I knew I'd regret my decision to wear a t-shirt and mini-skirt eventually. At the moment, I was all too aware that my skin must feel clammy to the touch. A sweaty film coated me from my earlier exertion.

At least I didn't care as much about the dank, cold, subterranean air as I would if I'd been sober.

In fact, my heart sang with joy at simply surviving after all that. My head swam with all the alcohol.

Annabelle broke our embrace and stood up to look around. She ran a hand through her hair to get it out of her eyes. "Holy crap, Skye! Is this the place? I can't believe any of this. I keep thinking I'll wake up, but I hope I don't, now that we're here."

I let out a whoop and windmilled my arms with glee. "I know, right? Just *look* at this place! We're not in Naptown anymore, that's for damn sure!"

"Is that... what the hell is that, Skye?" Annabelle pointed at a shaggy eight-foot mound of hair and long limbs that looked just a bit like a Wookie to me. It pulled a rickshaw full of adorable little bouncing rabbit people in waistcoats and pinafores.

"It's Chewbacca or it's Bigfoot, maybe? I haven't seen anything like this outside of my dream that led us here."

Annabelle shrieked and shook her leg. Some thing looking like a cross between a spider and a squirrel had climbed up to her knee. It chittered, and its black eyes shined. She scraped it off with the poker. The stench of burned hair stung my nostrils. The spider-squirrel screeched and scuttled away, twitched, then curled in on itself, dead.

"Eww," I said.

"You're a big help!" she said, whirling around to see if more of the nasty little things was lurking behind her.

"Let's move into the light, toward the market itself," I suggested.

She let me lead. I kind of wanted my poker back now, but I guessed Annabelle felt a bit more in control as long as she had it. And I had to admit, she wasn't as drunk as I was, and therefore could wield it more effectively than I could just then.

The market overwhelmed my senses. Lights and sounds and shapes and smells moved in bewildering patterns. The diversity of the crowd could put even your average Star Wars movie to shame. I had no idea what most of the vendors had for sale, but their shouts formed a roaring cacophony that washed over us like an ocean tide.

The first shops we came upon were only large blankets spread out on the ground. They were lit by paper lanterns of all colors, hanging on a crook planted in the clay. The lanterns flickered and glowed, lit by candles, I thought.

These shopkeepers were hunched little fellows, grayish-skinned, with long nails and heads that looked too big for their bodies. Their faces, flat and pop-eyed, reminded me of pug dogs. With cheery smiles, they sprang into action, dusted their wares, and danced about to catch our attention as we neared.

Something disconcerting happened when they talked. I could tell they weren't speaking English, but some odd growly babble instead. I still understood them through some means I didn't understand.

"Ho there, lovely ladies, come see my fine body ornaments!" crowed the nearest of these pug-goblins. "Things to wear on necks, wrists, ankles and tails! Pretty beads, mysterious gems, magical knots of flosses made from exotic materials! Come see, come see, they'll be yours for a song!" Annabelle drifted toward the merchant, curious. I felt a bit leery of talking to anyone but the merchant who held Minnie captive. Too late, Annabelle already crouched to look at the decorative strings.

"Hey, look at this one," she said, holding up a strand. It looked like it was made of silk cords, pea-sized black-lacquered beads and a few smooth but irregular gleaming hematite chunks. Before I could say anything, she tied it around my left wrist.

"See, a friendship bracelet!" she exclaimed, beaming up at me.

"You've an eye for the finer things, I can tell," the pug-goblin merchant purred. "It only adds to your friend's beauty and grace."

I snorted at that, but I had to admit that I loved the thought, and the bracelet was beautiful. It felt warm and soft against my wrist, not restricting or heavy.

I looked Annabelle in the eye, intending to say I couldn't accept it. I mean, who knew what they used for money here? She caught me smiling before I could stop myself, and our grins fed on each other.

"You know you like it," she said.

"But what does it cost?" I asked, looking at the merchant.

"Cost? What is cost if the heart desires it?" he danced a jig and wrung his hands with glee. "What have you to trade, hmm? Mortals from mortal lands, I'm sure you have wealth beyond imagining."

We both laughed, and the merchant's face fell.

Annabelle fished around in her pockets and came up with a keychain. Dangling from it was a blue Swiss Army knife, no bigger than my little finger. She detached it from the keys and offered it to the pug-goblin. "Trade ya?"

The merchant turned the knife over and over in his clawed hands, looking puzzled. Annabelle had to take it from him to show him how to open the knife, nail file, miniature scissors and bottle opener.

The knife delighted the merchant. "This is magic! I am shamed by your offer. I insist you find a second ornament, one for each of you!"

Annabelle waggled her eyebrows at me. I giggled and looked at the others laid out. Nothing black for my friend, no, she had enough of soot. But fire, now... I found a multicolored bracelet, its strands made up of orange, yellow and red. The bracelet had round beads that appeared to glow with a faint inner yellow-orange light, pulsing brighter and dimmer like candle flame.

I picked up my choice and tied it around her wrist as she had mine. I fumbled a bit at the knot, but though I thought it might slip, it was firm and felt permanent.

"Now you're mine," I teased, winking at her. *Oh my God, am I flirting with a girl?* Cold shyness and insecurity washed over me, and I couldn't meet her eyes.

She touched my chin to raise my face to look into her eyes. "And you can't get rid of me, either," she said, without a trace of humor in her voice.

The moment stretched out awhile, as I had no idea what to say in return. Should I kiss her? What did this mean anyway?

She broke the tension with a grin. "Bee eff effs!" Best friends forever. *That takes away the panic, but why do I feel let down?*

We pretended to punch each other in the shoulder and made silly faces.

The merchant bowed and thanked us and gushed about how beautiful we were with our new bracelets. We told him goodbye and continued on. The world swam around me, and I faltered, but she linked her arm in mine to steady me.

"We're off to see the wizard!" I sang.

"All right, Dorothy, tone it down a bit, we're attracting too much attention."

"Too much attention?" I waved a hand to encompass the crazy bazaar all around us. "Really?"

"You know what I mean! What are we looking for anyway?"

I described what I'd seen in the dream; the big lanky troll and his table, the jar of blue fire sprites, and the cage hung up that should have my Minnie in it. We peered around and did our best to ignore the sales pitches of the other blanket-sitting goblin merchants.

Annabelle shrieked and dropped the iron poker with a clang. I looked over to see her beating at a spider-squirrel that had climbed up onto her left breast. Another clung to her right knee, though I didn't think Annabelle had noticed it yet.

Annabelle flicked the breast-clinging spider-squirrel off her, and it landed on a goblin's blanket. A couple of bottles of glowing liquid tipped over but didn't break or spill. The goblin cursed at her, but grabbed up the squirrel spider and popped it in its mouth and chewed with a sickening crunching sound.

I didn't want to touch the disgusting creature, but I wanted to help, so I scraped at it with my sandal. It came off, but scrambled onto my foot and up my leg. I screamed and fell down in my panic to get it off me. I landed next to the poker, which I used to slap at the creature. The thing exploded as I hit it, sticky, charred bits of fur and flesh flying in all directions. I also whacked my shin with the iron poker hard enough to bring tears to my eyes.

The goblins' eyes narrowed at the sight of the iron tool, and I'd swear the temperature of the air dropped ten degrees in an instant.

There were more of the mutant fairy creatures, scuttling around us. More of them circled Annabelle. I used the poker to shoo them away, but they crept back when we turned away.

We found looking for the booth where Queenie had traded Minnie away much more difficult while fending off the spider-squirrel creatures. I grumbled in frustration, "What the hell's with these things, anyway?"

"I dunno, but they freak me out," said Annabelle, kicking one that had gotten too close with her sneaker. It curled into a ball and rolled underfoot and disappeared into the crowd.

The other patrons in the market were of all sorts—short, tall, human looking, animal-like or alien. Hair, fur, scales and feathers adorned heads that bobbed by. But the nasty little crawlers only came after us.

We hurried along to lose the spider-squirrel swarm in the crowd.

At last, a flicker of blue flame caught my eye and we rushed over to a booth that matched the one in my dream. Behind the table was the troll, just as I remembered. There were only two of the blue fire sprites left bouncing around in the jar now. He'd added another jar, this one filled with fireflies of the more ordinary sort, I thought. However, when I looked closer, I saw that these insects were itty-bitty winged people, glowing yellow-green with their own light. *What do you know, teeny fairies Walt Disney himself would appreciate!*

The little ones didn't look happy at all. Some of them pressed up against the glass as I peered inside, their mouths formed an O as they called to me, but I couldn't hear a sound.

Well, almost no sound. A soft buzzing and drone came from the jar, sad and melodic in its rhythm.

The troll's face appeared on the other side of the jar and his voice boomed at me. "You like? Their song is beguiling, is it not? Just a handful kept in your bedroom will give you the most wonderful sleep and erotic dreams as well."

I stared at him. The hundreds of little prisoners begged me to save them, flickering and fluttering between the stony troll's face and me.

"You have something of hers," said Annabelle, her voice as cold as I'd heard. She pointed up at the cage hanging from the tent behind him, covered with a muddy-colored canvas cloth.

The troll straightened to peer down at my friend. "Something she desires? Oh my yes, you will do nicely. Lavish payment indeed."

I gaped at the troll. "What? No. Oh no, I'm not trading my friend or anything for what's been stolen from me!"

"Come on, slimebag, hand over the cage," said Annabelle, backing me up. I felt so proud of her, standing up to a monster that way.

Then he laughed, deep, rich and long. The firefly people cowered on the bottom of the jar, and the blue fire sprites burned brighter and spun faster in their glass prison.

On sudden impulse, I picked up the jar with the fire sprites in it and held it over my head. "Give it up, tusk-face, or I use these guys as a Molotov cocktail on your tent."

His laughter calmed to a low rolling chuckle. "Threaten me and the price only goes up. Tell you what, girl, put down the jar and I'll haggle with you for that cage. You'll find no law here other than possession and trade, and I possess what you want. Let's trade."

I looked at Annabelle, who shrugged. I handed the jar to her. "I'll have my friend hold onto this as collateral for your goodwill, until I have my property back."

The troll didn't seem concerned, but instead held out his hands, palms up. "Tell me what you have to trade, other than this fine mortal?"

I felt sick at his suggestion of trading a *person* for anything, even a piece of myself. "I've got this nice iron poker, I've seen what it does to you guys."

Annabelle made a sizzling noise with her tongue behind her teeth.

The troll took a step back. "I thought we were trading. Believe me, I can defend myself. Deal is off. Good day."

I shook my head. "No, I meant to trade this for my property. It's got a wooden handle, you could hold that part and wield it yourself, like some kind of fairy lightsaber."

He spat on the ground between us. "Augh! You believe me to be an iron-handler? Unlike you, I have honor, mortal girl! And I would not use that word in this place, if I were you. It's an insult. Again, I say, no deal, good day."

He seemed to mean it. I had to come up with something of more value.

"Okay, okay, here's something else," I said, digging the pepper spray out of my purse. "This sprays a stinging chemical into the eyes of an attacker!"

He snorted. "As I said, I can already defend myself. I have no need of it."

I rummaged around some more. Nail polish? No. Bus pass? Forget it, I needed that, and it wouldn't do him any good. The Transit King's coin? No, I didn't think that'd be a good idea, not only might I need it, but I thought perhaps the King would take offense.

Then I found the pendant. The resin casting with the memory chip containing my earliest chat logs when Stuart and I were falling in love. What had Babette called it? Oh yeah. The soul of our relationship.

I guessed that was pretty much a wash now. But hey, maybe the shiny object would be worth a try with this goon.

I held it up, and in this place, the cheap resin glowed with a cool silvery light of its own, independent of lantern-light, the glow of the firefly people, and the swirling blue fire sprites. It was as though I held up an amulet made of moonlight.

The troll stared at it and asked if he could hold it. I let him. He held it up and sniffed at it. "This," he said in a hushed tone, "will do nicely. Do you give it freely for the cage?"

Didn't seem like I'd get a better offer. "Yeah," I said, still feeling sick, but excited now that Minnie'd be back with me in a moment.

He put the pendant into a jar that could have been used to store baby food and stowed it in his tent. I started to freak out, worried he'd renege on his end of the deal, but he brought the cage down with a hook and lowered it to my feet.

"Excellent haggling, little tart, now that you have what you came for, begone from my shop!" He made shooing motions with his hands.

Annabelle put the sprite jar back in its place, and I picked up the birdcage and backed away. I peeked under the covering to retrieve my Minnie.

I was greeted by the screaming face of a solitary blue fire sprite, spitting fire that singed the hairs on my arm.

I plunked the cage down on the table next to the jars and shouted, "What the hell?"

The troll scowled. "What now? No refunds!"

"This cage had a little version of me in it, a little person. Her name is Minnie, and she's mine. You tricked me, you bastard!"

He waved his hands in front of us. "Hey now, I didn't know your heart's desire, and you didn't ask to see before the deal was done. No refunds."

I picked up the jar with the firefly people in it and unscrewed the lid and freed them. They burst out in a glowing, gleeful crowd, and I found my face covered in bug-sized kisses. Then they swirled off into the night.

"Hey! That's my property you just let go!"

I held up the poker with what I hoped was menace. "And I'll destroy more of your property until you give me back my Minnie, you cheat."

He winced at the word *cheat.* "Look, okay, so I sold the thing before you got here."

"I don't believe you," I said, knocking the fire sprite jar to the ground. The glass crashed and the freed fire spirits stayed only long enough to free the third sprite in the cage. The covering smoldered and flickered with blue flames as they zipped off into the crowd.

"Stop that!"

"Tell us who you sold her to," said Annabelle, tone dangerous.

"Look, okay, customers expect confidentiality, but you paid a pretty penny, and I can't afford more trouble. So I'll just say that she got bought back by the same lady who sold her to me."

Oh no. Queenie!

"Skye, it's time to go," Annabelle grabbed the poker from me. She swatted at a spider-squirrel on my back, and it it sizzled and popped. I looked around and found we were surrounded by hundreds of the things, climbing over each other to get to us.

I'd gotten all I was getting out of the troll anyway.

Annabelle cut a stinking swath through them and they scattered on one side and backed up a bit on the others. "Let's go!" she said, taking my free hand with hers. She dragged me headlong through the crowd of the market, dodging and crashing into other patrons of all descriptions. I had one horrible moment when I collided with a walking snake. I know it's a girly stereotype, but snakes freak me out. It took a terrible, slick several moments to disentangle myself. Worst of all, the snake person seemed delighted to be coiled around me, and made a game of tripping me up. Gross!

The spider-squirrels pursued, hot on our tails. I had to kick at some of the faster, bolder ones as they caught up and tugged at my pant legs. I hated the feel and sound of the crunch they made when I stepped on them.

Not too soon for me, we passed the pug-goblins' blanket shops. Their cajoling cheers and whining pleas didn't slow us one bit. I dared to look back at that point.

I shouldn't have.

The sheer mass and roiling clambering of the spider-squirrels behind us made the hairs on my arms and the back of my neck raise in terror. I didn't know what they wanted, but I sure didn't want to find out.

Annabelle slowed a little and shouted at me. I was too preoccupied with not wetting my "oops" panties to make out what she said at first. She jerked on my arm to get my attention.

"Wake up, Skye! Which one is it?"

I looked away from the furry million-legged horde to see the roof rushing to meet the floor, making a wall ahead of us.

There were half a dozen cave mouths in the general direction from which we'd come.

"Oh my God," I said, not feeling very helpful. "Uh..,"

"We don't have much time!" my friend said, panic rising in her voice.

I scanned the area, trying not to panic. I thought to myself, *if Minnie were here, she'd know.*

Just then, I saw it. In front of the second cave mouth to our left lay the crooked, burnt body of the first spider-squirrel that we'd met. I made an incoherent noise and pointed, urging Annabelle toward it.

I no longer dared to look back. All I could hear was a squeaking, skittering, clicking rumble, like an earthquake made of flesh and bones, rolling toward us.

I pulled Annabelle down, but she made me go first, holding the little monsters off with the poker. The air smelled of burnt hair and flesh, and was filled with little screams, like mice caught in a glue trap.

I crawled into the cave and felt the tingling of static electricity. I moved inward, listening for Annabelle following me, and was able to crouch and walk faster and faster as the ceiling and walls expanded out and away from us. I thought of Holliday Park, and of the fairy circle in particular. I fixed an image of it in my head. I was still drunk, but the adrenaline that came from my fury at the cheating troll, and from the horrible tide of nasty little creatures pursuing us had me more alert and focused now.

Annabelle took hold of my purse strap to follow me single-file. The sparks shot from my feet and trailed from my fingers and hair as I walked, the resistance building up before me once again. They grew so great in density that we bathed in the white light of the vortex tunnel once more. The roar of the energies around us rivaled Niagara Falls in volume. I felt the energies course through me, burning away my earlier terror and anger and filling me with exultation of escape and raw power.

Annabelle was trying to call something to me from behind, but I couldn't make out the words. Also, we'd seen the danger of stopping earlier, and I didn't want to repeat that.

Almost, just for a half a second, the image of the horrible gibbering, oily black mouthing things threatened to distract me from my focus on our destination.

I tripped over my own feet, and almost fell, but Annabelle caught me and pressed her whole body against me from behind, helping me stay upright and walking. Her body heat reminded me of the warmth of the summer day waiting for us in the park ahead. I thanked her out loud, but my words were torn away from me by the winds and energies whirling around us.

The path curved, just a little at first, then into tighter and tighter spirals. The stones of the park faded into view once again, and my path wrapped around them, counter-clockwise this time. The vortex lost power bit by bit, and we saw through it's light in widening stripes as we slowed and arrived. I walked us three extra times around the circle until the sparks and winds guttered and died.

"We made it home!" I cried.

Annabelle whirled me around with one hand on my shoulder and stood on her toes. She slid her hand up to the back of my neck and pulled my face down to hers and kissed me full on the lips. She kissed me like she was nibbling and playing at first, then the tip of her tongue tickled my lips.

I found myself responding, trying not to have a certain Katy Perry song go through my head. I was already on a high from the escape and from the vortex energies, but this just sent me over the top. I didn't *care* that she was a girl; Annabelle's kiss made me feel so alive and wanted.

Now, I have to confess, I kiss with my eyes closed. I like to be carried away by the sensations. I love to lose myself in my lover's affections. But just then, I heard a twig snap, and I opened my eyes.

I wished I hadn't. My life might have been complete, had I only had just another hour or two to just enjoy that kiss, and well, I didn't quite know what would have followed.... But I opened my eyes and didn't get a chance to find out.

We were surrounded by sharp, pointy, glinting-tipped pikes, held by Her Royal Bitchiness' froggy foot soldiers.

They all looked pissed off, too.

I knew we'd had it, and the last thing I wanted my dear Annabelle to do was die for me. Not breaking the kiss, I slipped my fingers into the collar of my t-shirt, down into my bra. I pressed the transit token into Annabelle's hand and broke the kiss and looked her in the eyes.

"Think of your favorite place in the city," I said.

Shocked and surprised, she said, "What?"

Ignoring her question, I held her hand tightly around the coin and murmured, "Pick me up, pick me up, pick me up."

Annabelle opened her mouth to ask a question, but before she could speak, the spectral outline of a city bus flashed by, and she was gone.

So was the iron poker.

The far-off echoing of the bus's engine held a cackling laugh.

I shivered, despite the eighty-plus degree heat of the afternoon around me. I smiled at the thought that she sat on a bus somewhere elsewhere in the city, under the Transit King's protection.

I put up my hands as the frogmen's pikes poked me from all directions. I said, "I surrender, and I swear, for what it's worth, I've never eaten frog legs in my life!"

Chapter Seven

I wondered what I must look like to the normal people in the park as the big, bipedal, froggy soldiers marched me up the trails and out toward the stony castle. I hoped one of the picnickers, joggers, or frisbee-throwers would think a girl walking along with her hands in the air was suspicious. I *wanted* them to call me in for Public Intoxication. *Anything* to help me get away from these otherworldly creeps.

No such luck. People mind their own business unless something becomes a personal inconvenience. To them, I was probably just some weirdo drunk. Too bad this wasn't a Denny's in the wee hours. Someone always made it their business to complain if a bunch of us vampire types freaked them out, talking about the game. Scaring the straights, we called it. Great fun, but it wasn't working to my advantage here in broad daylight.

I thought about drawing more attention to myself, but if I so much as drew in a breath to speak, one of my amphibious escorts would poke me in the ribs with a silver-tipped pike.

Maybe if I start bleeding from a puncture wound, a kind citizen will call for help for me? Maybe not even then.

We passed the headless statue that flanks the faux ruins, and passed under some trees. A drawbridge was down, and the frogs prodded me until I crossed the bridge. I didn't see what choice I had, and I have to admit I was curious.

Inside was a courtyard that could host a basketball game with room to spare. The stone flags under my feet were an irregular mosaic of jagged chunks of flat slate. The sky above changed as we entered, nighttime now, rather than late afternoon. The moon lit the yard with a pale silvery glow.

I don't know how I missed her, but suddenly Queenie stood in front of me. The frog goons parted to present me to her. Her face was still a teenager's, features soft with baby fat, lips pouty and red. But instead of the jeans and stretch velour top she'd had on yesterday, she wore a long purple satin gown. To say her dress was low-cut would be to say the Grand Canyon was a "nice ditch". A bronze vine wound around her waist and her skirts almost swept the floor at her feet.

I had the bizarre urge to touch the fabric. I knew it'd feel cool and slick between my fingers.

Her cold eyes regarded me like she'd found a spider-squirrel stuck to the bottom of her sandal. I waited for her to say something, since she'd gone to so much trouble to bring me here. Hey, it was her party, but I wasn't feeling chatty at the moment.

"I could have you killed right now," came her oily words after a long pause. "Can you give me a good reason I shouldn't?"

"I'd make a terrible mess all over your nice castle yard here. I hear that, even if my blood doesn't go everywhere, the last thing my body'll do is void my bowels and empty my bladder all at once. You can clean and clean that kind of thing, but it just never quite goes away."

Queenie took three quick steps toward me and slapped my face so hard I heard bells and thought I saw the Death Star explode right there before my very eyes.

"What do you think this is all about, child?" her voice came from the grooves of an ancient vinyl record with an icicle for a needle. Her breath smelled earthy, like mushrooms.

"If I had to guess, you just couldn't get a date to the dance, so you burned down my house so you could ask Stuart to the Danse without fear of rejection." I had no idea why I was pressing my luck to this point. Maybe I had some kind of death wish?

She slapped me again. The bells rang out for Christmas Day once more. The courtyard spun and tilted.

"If you're going to do that, you could at least call me a whore and pull my hair a bit, so I can tell you what a naughty girl I am. Oh, and my safeword is 'mongoose'."

I shouldn't let vodka do my talking for me.

Still, I felt some satisfaction as her pale, cool face reddened with anger.

"You idiot. You don't know how close your prattling is to the truth. You are supposed to be dead now. Unfortunately, I have rules and customs to follow, so as much as I'd love to cut open your belly and tie you up with your intestines, I'll have to simply keep you here until the Danse is complete."

The Danse? The make-believe vampire politicking, veiled excuses to pair off and screw each other in private? Why would our game's celebration be of any importance to a fairy Queen? All I could imagine was the pageantry appealed to her, the costumes, the dancing, seeing and being seen....

It must be something about that group of people. Their extraordinary willingness to suspend disbelief might be it. What did Queenie want with my friends? What did she want with Stuart?

And, more immediate, what did she want with me?

I tried playing dumb. "I see, you're just threatened by my mad rock-paper-scissors skills. They are to be feared. But Queenie baby, the Danse Macabre is a social event. You can relax and just play your character, you know? It's great for newbies like yourself."

Her face twisted into something a lot more animal than human. The nails on her hands grew longer and sharper, and when she snarled at me, I saw sharp wolfish teeth. I admit I cringed, despite my bravado, as she raised her arm and lashed again at me with her hand. I raised my hand to block her attack out of reflex and found myself thrown backward and down, and landed hard on my butt.

I saw astonishment on her face and felt something similar myself, along with relief that those nails hadn't raked me.

"Throw her in the dungeon," snapped Queenie, her mouth full of teeth getting in the way of the command to her goon squad. The sharp metal tips of the pikes jabbed into me, urging me to my feet. Queenie swept away into the main building at the center of the castle walls.

Meanwhile, I was marched along to an out-building, a blocky brick and stone structure with just one door and no windows. The frogs opened the heavy wooden door with an oversized brass key. They took my purse away from me and pawed through it. I felt sick. Everything I owned, including my hotel room key, debit card, IDs, and my bus pass were all in that bag. All I had now were the clothes on my back and the jewelry I wore.

I clasped my hands in front of me to conceal my goblin market bracelet and silver rings as best I could. I doubted any of that would save me now, but I needed something to hang onto.

A couple of the froggies shoved me in the door, into the near-dark passageway. Doors went off to the sides, and a stone staircase descended into the ground ahead of me. Painful jabs in the back guided me to the stairs and down. As I followed them into the earth, a stench of sweat, urine, old rotting meat, and feces rose to meet me.

"Oh ugh. And I thought you guys stank. Whooo-eee!" I said, waving a hand in front of my nose. "When's happy hour here anyway? I could use a drink."

Nasty laughter came from the frogmen behind me as my only answer.

A horrible, gargling scream came from somewhere far down the passage. I shuddered as the sound stopped short.

The tunnels twisted and turned, and we passed cells all along the way. Oil lanterns hung on wide-spaced hooks, but they were no match for the gloom of the place. Narrow window slits at roughly the height of my shoulders provided brief, dim glimpses of occupants.

In one, I thought I saw the mismatched goth girl I'd met on the bus that'd taken me to the park. She was held in a cage inside the cell, the bars confined her to a space so small she could neither stand up nor fully lay down. She wept, but didn't look up as we passed.

Another cell held a ball of fur and teeth, about twice the size of a basketball. It gnawed on a pile of cleaned bones. I winced at the sound of its teeth cracking the bones to get at the marrow inside. The sick sweet stench of death and decay escaped that cell and I paused, despite prodding, to bend over and vomit on the dungeon floor.

I'm sure the pikes prodded me hard enough to draw blood, but I was faint and miserable as I hunkered there, my stomach clenched over and over in the dry heaves that followed. I wished for my vodka or some water to rinse the awful taste out of my mouth. When had I eaten last? Sometime last night, I guessed.

The guards let me crouch there for a long minute, then resumed their prodding. I cursed them and rose, shaking. Dizziness overcame me as I stood up. I blacked out and fell into nothingness.

I wondered if the frogs bothered to catch me.

At first, it was just dark, then colors swam around, reminding me of the goblin market lanterns. Then, the darkness brightened. I blinked in bright sunlight. I smelled sea salt and heard waves crashing. I had the impression of bamboo structures topped with grass thatching, people wearing clothes with loud colors lounged in wicker chairs. One woman on the end of the bar went so far as to sling her ta-tas in an actual coconut bra. *That can't be comfortable.* Somewhere out of sight, a cover band murdered a Jimmy Buffet song.

A tiki bar? How'd I get here? I blinked like a mole at the bright beach scene. At least I wasn't too out of place with what I wore. My skirt and t-shirt had been replaced with a wrap-around sari, which looked to me like it'd been made from cloth from an XXXL Hawaiian shirt. It was comfortable and light, and somehow familiar at the same time. I wondered if my underwear still said "oops". The answer came to me as I had a strange memory of putting on a bikini before the Hawaiian sari.

I took a step out of the shelter of the hut and realized my feet were bare and the sand squeezing between my toes was hot.

"Howdy, stranger," came a tiny voice to my right. And there, sitting cross-legged on a wooden bar stool, was my missing bit, Minnie.

My feet burned as I tripped my way over to her, and perched on the stool next to hers. "Wow, are you a sight!" I cheered. "I thought I'd lost you!"

Minnie smirked. "Well, actually, you did. I'm still held captive someplace, but we're still one person when you get right down to it. I like to think the sum of our parts make for a greater whole, though!"

"So how are we here?"

She chuckled. "Well, you must be asleep, and I'm passing the time by meditating, here in my happy place. Though with you here, this bar appeared. I was sunbathing up until just a few minutes ago."

"Guess it's something like a lucid dream?"

She nodded and flagged down the bartender. He turned out to be an animated skeleton. "Bring my sister here a daquiri, would you, Bones?"

Bones the bartender nodded and clacked his teeth together. I couldn't tell if he was grinning since all skulls looked that way to me. He busied himself with bottles, fruit juice, ice and a blender. I prefer mine on the rocks, rather than as an alcoholic slurpee, but hey, no arguing with free drinks.

At least I hoped the drinks were free, since I didn't have anything on me but my bikini, sari and the bracelet Annabelle bought for me. The bracelet caught Minnie's eye as I reached for my daquiri, served in a coconut shell. I thanked the bartender, who extended a bony hand palm up, waiting for payment. Oops.

Minnie came up with some extra large coins and flipped them over to clatter on the bar. Not free after all. Bones continued to grin (maybe) and scooped up the bronze-colored coins.

My little alter ego whistled and motioned for me to show her the black-and-hematite bracelet. I passed my frosty drink to my other hand and let her see the adornment as I sipped through a reed straw. The daquiri was lime and strong and just right for a hot day on the beach.

"My my, thats a pretty bangle you've got since I was gone. Did you and Stuart make up?"

I shook my head. "No, it's a present from Annabelle. She's a new friend. She saved me from the fire, she's a fire fighter."

Minnie smiled. "Well good for you! You can't see it, I'm sure, but this is from the shadow world. I can tell it's not dream stuff, and it's not from your imagination like your clothes. Not worth much in Shadow but it'll be interesting to see what it does in the 'real' world you live in."

"What do you mean, 'what it does?'"

She nodded, letting go my hand. "Yeah, the stones, material and weave, as well as the intent behind the gift, can have an effect. Luck, protection, stealth, even love..." She looked at me with narrower eyes.

"Love? Is Annabelle a friend, or a *friend?*" asked Minnie, standing up on her stool to peer at me.

"I... I don't know yet. She saved my life, and she came with me to try to rescue you, and...."

"You kissed her, didn't you?" Minnie asked.

I slurped more of my daquiri. She twirled a hand in the air to encourage me to come out with it.

"Okay yeah, I kissed a girl, and I liked it. Happy now?"

Minnie giggled. "Love it! See, there's more to you than you think."

"What's that supposed to mean?"

"Oh, nothing much. Look, this dream is about to fall apart. I'd go for a swim if I were you."

"But where are you, Minnie?"

"I'm not where you are, I can feel it. You'll find me, count on that. It's inevitable. All I can say is, it all revolves around Stuart somehow. And what you want."

She climbed down her stool, using the rungs like a ladder. I took a last slurp of my drink, which turned out to be empty.

I followed Minnie past the sunbathers, out onto the sun-toasted sand of the beach itself. We stopped once my feet stood on harder packed wet sand. The surf lapped at my toes. Minnie just shucked off the white smock she'd been wearing, and ran nude into the surf, giggling with delight.

Not to be outdone, I untied my sari and let it fall to the sand. My bikini turned out to be solid black and shiny. I felt sexy, standing there in the sun, but also very self-conscious. I waded in after Minnie and dove in to swim once the cool water reached mid-thigh.

As I submerged, I felt the water go cold and wash all over me, and it felt like the waves slapped my face over and over....

I woke to find myself in a stone cell, lying on a cot of some kind. Someone stood over me, flicked me with cold water and slapped my cheeks, not with cruelty, but insistent. The light in the room didn't reveal much about the person's features, but I smelled halitosis, male sweat and stale coffee.

"Stop, stop, I'm awake, I'm awake already!" I cried, and sat up, though I regretted it. My head throbbed, worse than the 'ice cream headache' from the dream-daiquiri. I liked it better at the tiki bar on the beach. I missed my Minnie already.

"Shush, she'll hear, or one of them frog guys will!" the voice was low but not deep, and the finger that touched my lips to quiet me was gentle but rough with callouses. I thought I felt the pressure of the tip of a nail as well. He was silhouetted against the feeble lamp light from the hall, seeping around the edges of the door and through the slit. I had the impression of someone wearing a fuzzy hat with pointy ears.

Oh! Could it be?

"Don't I know you from the bus, Wolfie?"

"Huh? Yeah, but, um..."

"What?"

"How'd you know?"

"Know what?"

"That I'm part wolf. Well, sometimes. Since, well, since she caught me."

Hmmm. "Is Queenie the 'she' in question?" I asked.

I barely saw him nod, there in the dark, though I still couldn't make out his face. "Only we don't call her that, she's Queen Howl to her property."

"Property? What's that mean? She owns you?"

"Yeah, pretty much. She lures you away and hunts you down with her wolves, and just when you're about to die, she gives you a choice. Die or serve her. I'm one of the kids who chose to live, but now she owns me." His voice shook with fear or anger as he told his story.

"Pretty sucky choice there. Isn't there any way out of it?"

"Not that I've heard. She can snap her fingers and turn us into beasts, one of the pack, then it's so hard to think, just...well, just being one of the pack is all you can do, all you want is to be part of the pack and to please her."

"Yeah? So why are you telling me this, Wolfie? Is it something that she wants?"

He shook his head. "No, she'd have me skinned alive and wear me as moccasins if she knew I was here. We've got free will as humans, just not as wolves."

"So why risk yourself for me? I'm just a stranger from a bus. Judging by the way Queenie's ruined my life over the past couple of days, I'm not one of her favorite people. Not that I'm not grateful for your company and all, but you should go, Wolfie boy."

"Well, she may own me and the others, but like I said, I have free will. And right now, you're not her possession, just her prisoner. If I get you free, it'll piss her off. That's about the only thrill I've got left that's my own, you know?"

"That's all? You're risking your skin to irritate your Queen?"

"That, and I need to ask a favor in return."

Oh no, here it comes. "What?"

"I want my freedom. I want to go back to being just a skate punk, flunking Geometry. I want the scariest part of my day to be risking texting in class, not losing control of my body and soul at someone's whim."

Sure, that'd be great, but how? "What makes me so special, why do you think I can do anything like that?"

I could *feel* his wolfish grin, even if I couldn't see it. "Because word gets around. Your man is just like me, one of hers. She owns him, body and soul, and if you ever want him back, you'll have to figure out a way. All I ask is, if you free him, you gotta free me too."

"Fair enough," I heard myself agree. How the hell am I going to do that? "So she's got Stuart?"

"By the balls," he said, and my heart sank further. Stuart'd been a dick to me after the fire because he'd been taken by Queenie. No wonder he'd had all those healed scars, despite all the blood. She'd spared him, and he'd chosen to serve her rather than die.

I wondered what I'd do in that same situation. I think I'd rather die than lose myself and become a puppet.

Damn it! I realized it'd be so much easier to hate him for being horrible toward me than if he did it because he couldn't help it. Or because he felt it protected me from her somehow. If so, it sure hadn't helped me so far.

"Okay, I'll do it. By the way, Wolfie, what's your name?"

"Deke. Deacon, if you're being formal."

We shook on it, and I felt kind of silly. I'd feel awful if I let the kid down and he stayed a slave to Queenie. And Stuart? Well, he'd been good to me for years, and I still loved him, even after how things had ended. I owed it to him to free him, if only to see if we had a chance after all.

Deke handed me something. My purse! I could have kissed him. If I'd still been drunk, I probably would have, halitosis and all. I slung the big bag over my shoulder and stood. Sober or not, I felt dizzy still, and my stomach gnawed at itself with hunger.

Oh well. Time for a drink.

The vodka bottle wasn't in my bag. Neither was my pepper spray. My wallet contained my bus pass and debit card and my room key. That was a relief. I rummaged through the other random crap in there, and came up with my flask!

Precious....

I unscrewed the top, but cursed when only a few drops spilled out onto my tongue. Empty! Damn. I screwed the cap back on and put it back.

"How's this work?" I asked Deke.

"I'm going to slip out, leaving your door open a crack. Count slowly to...oh, a hundred should do. I'll distract the guards and you make a break for it. The drawbridge was down, last I saw."

What will I see when I leave this place sober?

No matter. I just wanted out.

Without another word, he left me. The door opened a bit wider, then not quite shut. A thread of flickering orange light betrayed the tiniest opening around the edges.

I remembered to start counting. *One Mississippi, two Mississippi....*

A guard flapped past my cell, grunting and croaking some kind of complaint to itself. Its pike rapped on my door as it passed. I held my breath, but the thick wooden door didn't budge on its hinges, even after being struck.

Forty-five Mississippi, forty-six Mississippi...

I heard distant shouting and growling coming from the hall. It grew in volume, and I heard thumps and croaks and the clatter of a dropped wooden pole.

Seventy-eight Mississippi, seventy-nine Mississippi...

Silence ruled the hallway, even more than before. No screams or whining came from my fellow inmates. I finished counting and crept to my door. I peered through the slit and saw nothing but the far wall, lit by the dim, flickering lamp light.

I slid my fingers around the edge of the door and pulled. The door, heavier than I thought, didn't budge. I put more and more of my weight behind it until the door flew open with a rusty screech and a loud bang as it hit the wall and bounced back, groaning the whole way!

If the guards didn't hear that, then frogs don't have ears. Ear-holes. Whatever frogs hear with.

I had to block it with my body to keep it from shutting again. For what it was worth, I kept from crying out as I was smashed between the hefty door and the stone wall.

Once the door stopped again, I decided to just press on. I peeked into the hall. No one and no thing appeared in either direction, just the hall, more cell doors, and a lamp in the distance. I put my sandals in my purse so I could move quieter, then padded down the hall in the direction Deke went.

The hall wound around, with a few branches, but I stuck to the widest passageway, since it looked the most familiar. I passed a damp patch on the ground and realized that this must be where I'd gotten sick. Someone had mopped it up. Good. I thought with spiteful cheer at the idea of the frogs having to clean up my mess.

I smelled the stench from the bone-chewer's cell and held my breath until I was past. It wouldn't be long now, I thought, and I'd be outside. Just a run through the courtyard and over the drawbridge....

Then I heard the soft sobbing from the goth girl in her cell as I passed. I couldn't leave her here to suffer and maybe meet the same fate as Stuart and Deke and the others.

I peered inside and saw that she'd been let out of the confining cage, perhaps to sleep.

"Hang on," I whispered into the slit of her door. "I'm going to try to spring you out of here, but you have to be quiet, okay?"

The sobbing stopped, and I heard her scuff her way to the door. Her eyes appeared in the slit, red and streaked underneath with the black of her mascara running. She started to say something, but I held my fingers to my lips and shushed her.

I rummaged in my purse and came up with a safety pin and a flimsy nail file. I didn't have much of an idea of how to pick locks, but these things were old and huge, like ancient skeleton key locks. I poked around inside with the file and the opened pin and felt things move around.

The bolt refused to slide back. I could feel time passing, and my window of opportunity to escape was slipping away with each Mississippi.

"Please," she said, "I'm scared. It was just a game. My mom's going to be so pissed if I don't get home by dinner. These people are crazy!"

I hushed her again, and then rummaged around again in my purse. Down at the bottom, something clanked against my empty flask. I pulled it out and held it up to look at in the dim light.

A brass key! *Looks like Deke supplied me with a backup plan.*

It fit in the lock, and though I think I bruised my fingers with the effort of turning back the bolt, I had it open, and found myself with my arms full of grateful teenage goth. At least she smelled a lot better than Deke.

I impressed upon her the need for quiet, and she took off her boots and tucked them under an arm, and she tiptoed along in her socks behind me.

We reached the stairs and climbed one step at a time, pausing every two or three to listen. When we reached the top, I had to hold back a scream as there were two frogmen sitting there. Goth girl didn't hold back, she let out a screech so high I thought all the dogs for blocks around would start barking.

No movement from the froggies. They had cups in front of them, and now that we sat still, I heard faint phlegmy snoring coming from the guards. The ability to sleep sitting up seemed like a good skill to develop for their career.

Goth girl and I didn't need a written invitation. We passed the snoozing guards and pulled open the door and took off running. Turns out, not all the guards were asleep. I heard croaking calls of alarm as we made our way across the courtyard.

"Come on, run!" I cried to my new companion as we pelted toward the drawbridge.

Chains clanked and hinges creaked, and the bridge rose.

The guards huffed and puffed as they flapped from other posts toward us. I was grateful none were between the bridge and us, and we reached it before they did. We ran up it as it became a ramp, and at the end, I helped lower the goth girl to the ground, urging her to jump. She made it!

A pike whistled past me, hurled by one of the frog guards at the base of the drawbridge. I looked down ahead of me. The lip of the bridge now hung over the moat, and I had to hang on to keep from sliding back down as it continued to rise.

I couldn't do anything else, so I leaped out over the moat, screaming like an idiot as I fell.

I landed hard on one foot, and I felt my ankle twist and pop, but didn't feel the pain yet. I fell, but my teenage friend pulled me up and we ran together toward the exit of the park.

I turned around and looked, and to my surprise, I failed to see the castle, just the faux ruins that I ought to see there. I didn't see the frogmen, but as I turned back forward, I caught the glint of a pike out of the corner of my eye.

Great. Now they're after us, but even I can't see them.

I almost fell several times as we ran for the exit. The pain of my sprained ankle had started to reach my brain, and it wasn't fun to put weight on it. My newest friend helped me along as best she could, but I knew we'd be caught again at any moment. After that escape, I doubted we'd just get thrown in prison. Queenie would make us suffer, and maybe I'd find out what I'd do, given the choice of life or serving her.

Or maybe I wouldn't even get that choice.

Chapter Eight

So of course, I tripped again. My poor friend fell when I did, but she was determined, and I found myself being dragged along.

"Hey help me up, come on!" I yelled. I admired her energy, but I couldn't imagine we'd make progress this way. I could just imagine the invisible frogmen all around us. Was that depression in the grass behind us from our footsteps? Maybe, I imagined, it was big and flat like a froggie's flipper. If so, it was already too late.

Giving up would be the only swifter way for it to be over.

She helped me up, but continued to pull at me. I hopped and winced and stumbled my way along. I knew I heard something now, and I caught flashes here and there, and glimpses of purple or greyish green color out of the corners of my eyes. My heart pounded, my breath came short as I fought back panic.

That's when I saw it.

"Make for the sign! Go, go!" I saw the bus stop sign ahead of us. My un-named goth girl friend looked at me like I was crazy. "Your getaway car is a city bus?" she panted, just about yanking my arm out of its socket to keep me from tripping once again.

"Trust me," I said, not feeling as confident as I tried to sound. "I've gotten you this far, haven't I?"

She sighed and we kept on, getting a rhythm going, sort of like a three-legged race. I felt the ground thud behind us, as unseen footfalls gained on us step by step.

We got within ten feet of the bus stop sign when I fell again, hard, on my knees. I cried out in pain. An instant later, something slimy had a hold of my bad foot. That something twisted, and I screamed. "Drag me to the sign!" I cried.

Goth girl grabbed my hand, and I was in a tug of war. I had no doubt who'd win in a fair fight, but I didn't feel like fighting fair. I kicked with my good foot at the air. The first kick missed. I looked away, and in my peripheral vision, I made out the vague lumpy form of one of the frog guards, hanging onto me and slobbering. I could tell there were others close by.

The next kick hit him in his bulbous eye, and I felt a disgusting but quite satisfying pop. He let go, and my friend fell over backwards as I was freed, and we were both propelled the last few feet to the bus stop sign. I scrambled on hands and aching knees to the base of the sign and grabbed it with both hands.

"Asylum!" I cried. "I request asylum from the Transit King for me and my friend!"

"Hannah," said my friend, putting a hand on the sign post, looking around in a panic.

"What?"

"That's my name. Hannah," she said with a bit of a whine.

"Oh. Sorry. Didn't get your name on the bus, or just now while we ran for our lives, so sorry," I said, sounding bitchy to my own ears. I felt sorry right away. *I've had better days than this one. Cut me some slack, okay?*

"I know, I know, sorry. Just thought you should know before we, like, die and stuff."

I pulled myself up to a sitting position and looked around. I saw flat spots all around us in the grass, and I smelled the sewer smell of many frog soldier bodies. They didn't approach closer than where I'd kicked the one, but stood in a semicircle around us.

"Listen, we're not going to die, but do you have a dollar seventy-five in exact change?" I asked Hannah. "It's kind of important."

"Uh, no. They didn't let me keep anything but my clothes in there," she replied, continuing to look at me as though I had sprouted an extra nose.

"It's just that... well, let me look," I rummaged in my purse. The froggies hadn't taken much, to my surprise. I found a couple of single bills. But I knew the drivers weren't allowed to take anything but exact change. I came up with a quarter and several pennies on my first scoop. I threw the pennies back in, since I knew the till on the bus only took 'silver' coins. I reached back in and came up with what could be the same pennies plus a dime.

I like the sort of randomness of having a purse big enough to carry a couple of full-grown cats. There's something cool about the idea that just about anything could be in there. It's sort of an extra-dimensional space of randomness. The bad part of that is that while most anything could be in there, it also means that coming up with something specific I need right now is much less likely than something I haven't seen in years.

So, I came up with a hairbrush, some long lost lipstick (I'd need that for the Danse!), the condom from the same sardine tin my underwear came in, a granola bar (food!) and the tangled wires of a pair of earbuds.

I heard the pneumatic sigh and squeak of bus brakes. I looked up and saw the number 28 bus rumbling its way toward us, its blinker on to make the turn.

Except it'd be across the street from our stop. And I only had singles and forty-five cents in change. Well, plus my own bus pass. One of us could make it, but not the other. And neither of us would at all unless we crossed the road to the other stop.

Maybe, just maybe, the frogs wouldn't act if they had witnesses. Especially witnesses from a bus, a rolling fiefdom of the Transit King. I'd have to figure out the fare issue too, but one thing at a time.

"Okay, Hannah, I need you to follow my lead on this exactly, okay?"

She nodded.

"First, take my bus pass. I'll want it back if we both get out of this," I said, waiting for her nod, to be sure she understood. "Okay, take my hand and hold on. Now stretch as far as you can to the road. That's it." I kept one hand on the sign and one in hers as we stretched as far as we both could. One of her sneakers was out in the lane, and a SUV driver glared at her, waiting for her to cross.

The bus squealed to a stop at the intersection, its turn signal blinking.

"Okay, see the other bus stop sign? Let go of me and run for it. I'll keep them busy, you stall the bus driver, okay?"

She didn't even pause to acknowledge, but dashed out into the road. A car screeched its brakes as it stopped to avoid hitting Hannah. My friend gave the driver a dirty look. Drivers forget that pedestrians always have the right of way, and often just don't pay attention.

Once she was across, the car passed her and the bus began its turn. She waved the bus pass at the driver like a magic talisman that would force the massive vehicle to stop.

I took one last look around me. The grass around me waved in a soft breeze, all except for a dozen or more flat spots only a few feet from me. The diesel smell of the bus wasn't enough to overpower the froggy stench, not at this close range. If I did this wrong, I'd be screwed.

Screwed, nice choice of words. Oh. There were worse things than simple capture at stake here.

The bus came to a full stop and hissed and "knelt" down. It was now or never. I let go my fingers and hopped and hobbled my way across the street. Another jerk honked at me. Despite the fear of imminent capture, I flipped the driver off without looking.

"Asylum!" I cried again. "I beg asylum!" I made it across the street, but as I breathed easier, the bus doors shut.

I had to pound on the side of the bus as I made my way along its side to the door, crying "Asylum!" the whole way.

I heard squeaks and noises inside the bus, and just when I thought it was taking off, the driver took pity on me and opened the door. Hannah stood there, arguing with the man. Good Girl. It was more one-sided than an actual argument, as the turbaned guy with the beard behind the wheel tuned her out pretty well.

"Hey George," I said, recognizing the driver. He grunted and nodded at me and pulled the lever to shut the door. It didn't shut all the way, and I could hear a wet, slapping, scrabbling noise.

"I said, Asylum!" I cried as I grabbed George's hand and slammed the door on the frog guard over and over. I heard a croaking squeal and the door shut.

George looked me up and down, glaring at me with irritation in his eyes.

"Sorry, I was just helping," I said, taking my hands off the lever and his hand.

"Maybe you do need an asylum," said George with a dangerous tone, "but this bus is going away from the hospital, not toward it, Skye." On a normal day, I found his accent charming, but right now, that cross edge I heard made me worry even more about my lack of exact change.

The bus rolled away from the curb, much to my relief, but George demanded payment. Hannah stood there looking helpless. She handed my bus pass back to me, but I knew it couldn't be swiped twice. I held up my two dollars and forty-five cents.

"Exact change!" snapped George. "Or you get off at the next stop. You know better."

Hannah came to my rescue. In her saddest, lost little girl voice, she pleaded with the passengers. "My friend needs exact change, won't someone help her?"

My fellow passengers pretended not to hear at first, stony looks staring straight forward, right through us.

I added, "I'll give a dollar forty-five for three quarters!"

Now they heard me. People rummaged in pockets and purses. After a moment, we traded for quarters with a tiny woman with a heavy Hello Kitty backpack. She smiled, as though we were pals because she did me the favor of taking my money.

George flipped the sign on to show the bus was stopping. I fed my dollar and quarters into the hopper and listened to them clatter down inside. George gave me another look of warning, but motioned for Hannah and me to sit down. "Get behind the line," he growled.

The bus had plenty of single empty seats, but we opted to go all the way to the back so we could sit together. As soon as my butt hit the seat, I started to shake, and hot tears blurred my vision. I held up my hands to hide my face and hated myself for bawling in public again. I kept my crying silent, but I shook and knew everyone could see. I felt Hannah pat my shoulder.

I let it run its course. I cried for Stuart, torn from me by Queen Bitch and enslaved. I cried for all my efforts to rescue my Minnie coming to nothing but pain. I cried out of hunger and exhaustion and loneliness. I cried out of embarrassment, making a scene like this on a public bus. I even cried because I hated feeling sorry for myself.

Hannah nudged me. I wiped my eyes with the backs of my hands and peered at her. "Huh?"

She handed me a bottle of water. I needed it, so I cracked it open and drank half of it down in long gulps before coming up for air. It wasn't cold, but it felt so good going down. I thanked Hannah. She shook her head and pointed to a little guy that sat on the other side of her. "It's from him. He says his name is Bask?"

The Transit King had joined us. He grinned at me and tipped his aluminum foil crown at Hannah. "Evenin' ladies! Glad to see you made it out all right. Nasty piece of work, she is."

"How do you know about what happened?" I asked.

The little King chuckled and slapped his knee. He thumped his feet against the front of the seat, his feet far from touching the floor. "Not much goes on in these buses or along their routes that I don't get wind of, to be sure. Speakin' of wind, you two smell like a stretch of bog."

Great. I was Stinky Bus Girl again for the second time in one day.

Then something occurred to me. "Did she, I mean my friend...?"

"Oh yes, the wee firefighter popped onto one of my chariots up near Castleton a few hours ago. She's safe as houses, I made sure o' that for ye. Didn't think ye'd give my token to another. Must be someone awful special, I'll warrant." The Transit King winked at me.

"What are you *talking* about?" asked Hannah, interrupting my next question.

I looked at the little man and he shrugged, showing me his palm and tilting his head to one side. Guess I get to explain.

"This is the Transit King, he rules the buses of Indianapolis," I said.

"King Bask, if you're wantin' more of a name than just a title," he added.

"So, let's get this straight," Hannah said, measuring out her words one at a time. "You think you're some kind of a King, and that psycho Queenie thinks she's a real Queen?"

King Bask's eyes twinkled. "Anyone can be royalty, if they can defend their title and get others to follow."

Hannah eyed King Bask with suspicion. I didn't care what she believed, or even whether the King and Queen titles meant more than the titles my vampire gamer friends gave themselves. I owed more than just a favor to Bask, there's no way Annabelle, Hannah or I would have escaped Queenie without his help.

"Thank you, King Bask," I said, "for what it's worth, you've got my support."

The little King let out real belly laugh. It surprised me that no one on the bus turned to look. "Thank ye, lass. And I've another surprise for ye."

He handed me a business card. On it was a name, a title. Annabelle Cicero Adams, IMPD volunteer. There was a phone number and email address as well. "Yer friend asked that I get this to ye. She wanted to take the next bus back to Holliday Park, but I advised her against that just now."

I rummaged in my purse and was amazed to find that my cell phone hadn't been filched by the froggies. I punched in the number and waited, heart pounding as it rang.

I was so relieved when she picked up and said, "Hello?"

"Annabelle! I got your card from my friend. I escaped Queenie and I'm on my way downtown."

"Thank God! I was terrified you were dead or captured, sweetie! I'm already downtown, the little guy told me I should wait. Want to meet me for a bite to eat?"

"You have no idea how hungry I am. That's the best idea I've heard all day. How about I meet you at that brewpub off of the Circle? My pal, Heath, is the brewmaster."

"Gotcha, babe. On my way, see you when you get there!" Annabelle hung up.

"Greg Heath?" asked King Bask.

"Uh, yeah," I said, a little put off that he'd be so blunt about eavesdropping. "Know him?"

King Bask flashed me his impish grin. "O' course! No one makes Elderberry Stout like Mr. Heath. You could say he has a way with beer that I've not seen in a mortal since I left the old country."

I wondered if there'd been buses in his old country back then. Before I could speculate out loud, my young friend butted in and said, "Hey. This is my stop, my parents are going to throw a fit about losing my cell phone and being late for dinner. I'll see you at the Danse tomorrow, Skye, thanks again."

Hannah pulled the cord to request her stop and patted my shoulder in thanks, then she was out the door.

The Transit King murmured to me as the doors shut and we resumed our trip. "Didn't want to say while she was here, but that girl Hannah? I believed her to be workin' for Queenie. I don't doubt she'll be reconsiderin' her allegiances now! But just take care what ye tell her, lass."

Hannah? An agent of Queenie's? Then what was she doing in the dungeon like that? Come to think of it, though, she even mentioned Queenie the first time I'd seen her.

"So, about that favor," said King Bask.

Uh oh.

"Seein' as me token saved yer pretty girlfriend, and seein' as asylum on me bus saved yer bacon, I figure my end's been held up. Yer allegiance means much, and I'm sure we'll be useful to each other, but I have to ask the favor."

He called Annabelle my girlfriend!

"Well, she's not exactly...," I began.

"Tut tut, don't be worryin' about what ol' Bask thinks of ye. Yer sweet, savin' yer friend before yerself, lass. Very noble, like yer family MacLeod before ye. Me favor is this: Queenie's plannin' somethin' for that Danse Macabre your friends have goin' on tomorrow night. She has somethin' that belongs to me. She can't hold it herself, so one o' her lackeys'll have it. If ye can get it for me, we'll be even. If not, at least get me what information ye can, all right?"

I had a sinking feeling about this. "Well, I can try...what is it?"

"See, yer special, aren't ye, lass? Ta anyone else, it'll be disguised. A maraca, a champagne flute, a carpenter's hammer...something ye can hold in one hand. But you...well, we both know there's a bit o' ya in my world, so ya can see things for their true natures."

"Under the right circumstances, yes. I have to be tipsy," I admitted.

He chuckled. "Interestin'. Well, ye get yerself a wee nip and ye'll see it's a sceptre, a polished wood baton capped on both ends with silver an' gems inset. Got it?"

I nodded. "I'll do my best."

He clapped me on the knee with one of his hot, sweaty hands. I tried not to flinch at the uninvited contact. "If ye can sneak out o' Queen Howl's fortress and rescue a damsel in distress as you go, then you're a right hero, you are! You've proved yerself fit to be my agent, lass."

Despite the creepy way he tended to invade my personal space, I felt myself swell with pride at this endorsement. *A hero? Me? Aw, shucks.*

"Now go to your lady, me love. Ye'll want someone to watch yer back, especially if ye've got to be tipsy to see true." He pulled the cord and the STOP REQUESTED sign dinged and lit.

I was surprised to find that we were downtown already. As the bus slowed, I asked King Bask, "One more thing. Do you know where Queenie might have hidden Minnie, the bit of my soul she stole?"

The Transit King frowned as the brakes squealed, slowing the city bus to a stop. "Ye got me on that one, but I'll put out me eyes and ears ta see what I can find out when ye find me that sceptre."

Ah, more incentive. I searched his scruffy face for signs of trickery, but decided that either way, he'd given a sort of word.

As the doors slid open, I stood and pressed my luck. "Promise?"

He grinned and winked. "My promise is as good as yours, lass. You try your best and I'll try me best!"

I decided that'd have to do. "Thanks again, your majesty. Safe travels!"

Maybe I was buying too much into this, but hey, I pretend to be a vampire for fun, so I guess it's just in my nature to get in the spirit of the game.

I bounced down the steps and out onto the sidewalk. I felt a bit dizzy, even though I'd been sober since I escaped. My stomach told me why. I walked a block to the Circle, the Indiana Soldiers and Sailors Monument looming up ahead of me at its center. The phallic Monument rose up a couple dozen stories, surrounded by steps and giant statues, entrances visible at its base, both to climb up inside and to an underground museum. I've been up in the top observation deck, it's pretty neat.

I had to walk a quarter of the way around the Circle, past an ice cream and coffee place, whose strong, delicious aromas called to me with a power that threatened to pull me inside with a physical force.

I resisted, holding Annabelle and Heath brews in mind to counteract the siren smells. Soon, the understated Heath Brewery sign came into view, and I picked up my pace.

The blast of air-conditioning that met me at the door raised goose bumps on my arms and legs. The guy at the host's station made me clear my throat so he'd raise his eyes above my neckline.

"I'm looking for a friend," I began.

"Aren't we all, dear?" he quipped. I couldn't stop myself from smiling and blushing just a little at the flirt.

"Aren't you a doll?" I asked, buttering him up. "But I meant my..." I paused and decided what to say next. *Well, why not, just to knock this guy down a peg, for fun.* "...girlfriend," I finished with a wink.

The dear boy looked disappointed. "You're Skye, I'm guessing," he said, "Your friend's already in that booth in the corner."

He led me over to Annabelle, who leaped up out of her seat to hug me so tight that I couldn't breathe for a couple of heartbeats. I hugged her back, feeling relief and happiness wash over me.

Once she let me go, we both slid into the booth. The seat was sort of a horseshoe shape that curved around our table. We sat close together so we could talk without being overheard.

A server arrived with a big tray. To my surprise, he set a basket of chicken tenders and fries in front of me, a salad off to one side. Annabelle was given a plate that was dominated by a massive cheeseburger and fresh fried chips.

We each received a tall mug of cloudy white beer, garnished with orange slices.

"You are a goddess," I said, stuffing blazing hot french fries into my mouth.

She blushed. "Well, you said you were hungry. I gambled on what you might like, I didn't figure you're a vegetarian. Are you?"

I shook my head and washed the fries down with a blissful gulp of the Heath Brew. It was some kind of wheat beer, maybe a Belgian wit. Although any sustenance would be heaven, as hungry as I felt, Heath's stuff is my favorite.

Annabelle ate with me in silence awhile. I was sort of impressed at how she tucked away that burger. I don't know where she put it, she's just so small and cute.

We didn't talk about much of anything until after a beer refill came for each of us. I looked up and recognized they'd been delivered by Greg Heath himself. I jumped up and gave him a quick hug and kiss on the cheek. Greg's a little shorter than me, has a Roman nose. He's very fit too, lacking the beer belly that's just about universal in his profession.

"Hey, Skye. Good to see you. Sorry to hear about your place. You okay?" Greg's not a big talker, and this brief expression of sympathy was the gushiest I'd ever seen the man.

I sighed and shrugged. "Doing as well as can be expected. Did you hear from Stuart, then?"

He nodded. "Yeah, he came by earlier, on some vamp gal's arm."

Queenie. Greg's not in the vampire game himself, but he's into strategy games and stuff like that. He knows other gamers and he's always welcomed us, even in full freaky regalia, in his pub. It's endeared him to our crowd, and I've made it a point to show him we appreciate it. Stuart never appreciated the way I tease and flirt with Greg, but he put up with it since he can be outrageous with the vampire girls. All "in character" of course.

Anyway. "He was, hmm? Did they talk trash about me?"

Greg looked surprised. "No. Stuart just said you'd freaked out after being pulled from the fire and took off."

"He didn't try to tell you I started the fire on purpose?"

Greg's brow furrowed. "No, nothing like that."

Hmm. Curious. "Okay. Well, I guess he's cooled off a bit, maybe he wasn't himself this morning."

Greg nodded. "Yeah, bound to happen after something big like that."

Annabelle coughed. Oh yeah.

"Greg Heath, this is my new best friend, Annabelle. She's the one who saved my life this morning. She's a firefighter!"

They shook hands, and I sat back down next to Annabelle. I thought about it a moment, then took a chance. "Hey Greg, do you know a guy named Bask?"

Greg quirked a half-smile at me. "Yeah, that little guy owes me on his tab."

I laughed. "Seems like it's good to be owed by Bask," I said. "Beats owing him, at least."

Annabelle nudged me in the ribs, and I caught her winking at me.

Greg shrugged. "He's good for it. Why d'you ask about him?"

"Eh, I just ran into him on my way here and he complimented your Elderberry Stout and your brewing skills."

Greg snorted. "He should, he's had enough of it on that tab. Though he's had some good ideas for some of my private projects."

One thing about Greg is that everyone knows he loves beer experimenting more than anything else. If you showed even passing interest in trying something unique, he'd bring samples of his smaller batches.

I'd tried his beers made with sage, clove, juniper and all sorts of fruits. Most were at least interesting; several had turned my mood in a different way than beer alone. It's hard to explain, but Greg is a scholar of historical brews, many of which were supposed to have healing or inspirational properties.

Now, if a fairy King gave him tips, that'd be something worth trying. "So have you got anything around using his advice?"

Greg brightened. "As a matter of fact, I've got some special Heather Gruit ale for you to sample. It's not on the menu. I only made five gallons. Be right back. Nice to meet you, Annabelle."

I turned to pick up my mug of beer and found Annabelle staring at me. "What? Is there something on my face?"

"No, it's just you.... When I met you, my heart went out to you because you were such a mess, you'd lost everything. I just wanted to take you home and keep you, like a stray."

I felt my face get hot. Her words, though intended to be sweet, didn't strike me right. I looked away and murmured, "You didn't meet me on my best day."

"No, I didn't, Skye," she said, taking my hand in hers. I looked back into her steady, soft gaze. Annabelle blurred a bit before me as bitter tears welled up. She went on, saying, "You've been incredibly brave, you probably saved my life a couple of times to the once I saved yours. Just seeing you around Heath, I can tell there's a lot more to you than the person you seemed this morning. I kissed you then out of pity, but that kiss on the hill...well, that was real, and it was both of us, wasn't it?"

I nodded. "Yeah, and you should know, I've never...."

She put a finger to my lips. "And I'm not saying I know the future, but whatever else happens, I know I want you in it. We can take the rest as it comes."

I sniffed and nodded and wiped at the corners of my eyes. "Annabelle, I want to ask you something," I said, keeping my voice as steady as I could.

She didn't answer, but just watched me.

"Would you go to the Danse Macabre with me tomorrow night? It's a totally dorky vampire gaming thing...."

"Yes, I'd love to!" she said, before I could ramble on anymore.

I giggled. What is this, junior high school all of a sudden? "I want you there to help me, since Queenie will be there and I owe King Bask a favor, and it could be more trouble than even at the goblin market," I stammered out.

She looked at me a long moment. "And?"

"And you'd be part of the game too, it's fun but weird to an outsider. But I trust you, and I need your help. And, well, I want you there as my date, too."

She smiled and squeezed my hand. "You got it, babe."

I was about to lean over and kiss her right there in front of everyone, when Greg arrived. He slid into the booth with us, and put some little tasting glasses in front of all three of us.

"Okay, so this is the Heather Gruit ale. You can be taste testers, I'm thinking of brewing up a big batch and putting it on tap if enough of my regulars like it. It'll probably be better in the Fall or Winter, but...well, just try it."

Greg's too good a friend for me to be very annoyed at him for interrupting a moment. Still....

We each picked up a little glass of deep brown beer. I sniffed it, and found that it smelled earthy and spicy. I sipped, and the sweetness reminded me of gingerbread. It was bread-like and complex and had a hint of flowers about it.

"Wow what's in this?" said Annabelle, swirling the remaining half of her brew around her tasting glass and sniffing at it again.

Mona Lisa would be jealous of the mysterious smile Greg gave her. "Trade secret, ma'am, but I'll say that the name gives away the heather honey and heather flowers I used, among other things."

I found that my tasting glass was empty. Not only that, but I felt...different somehow. Everyone around me had taken on a glow. Annabelle had a soft yellow-orange aura surrounding her, while Greg's was a rich amber glow. Our server walked by, and he shined a bright lavender color. An elderly couple a few booths over seemed to share a dim aura of sea green.

Then I saw something else. I choked back a cry of surprise and dismay. Greg looked at me, brows knitted together. "Skye, if you don't like it, you can just say so."

Perched on an empty table across from us was what looked like a silvery glowing hologram of that damned gargoyle from my hotel room.

Chapter Nine

Without thinking, I grabbed a fork off the table and hurled it at the outline of the gargoyle. To my amazement, I struck it, producing a sharp bell-like tone as it bounced off the thing's stony skin.

It hissed and leaped from the table and scrabbled on the hardwood flooring toward the door, knocking over our server. His tray full of beer mugs went crashing and splashing to the floor.

"What the hell...Skye?" said Greg. He didn't raise his voice, but I'd never heard him so irritated.

I pointed at the fork on the floor. "Did you see that bounce off of nothing? I saw something there, a gargoyle. It was spying on me. Sorry about the mess...."

Greg looked from me to Annabelle. She shrugged. "I know it sounds crazy, but if you'd had the day I've had with her, you'd be smart to believe her. She sees things we can't, if she's a bit tipsy." She thought a second and added, "and not pink elephants or anything. You tell him, Skye."

I sighed at the look Greg gave me. "I think it's your Heather Gruit, it seems to enhance the effect, even just a small amount of it."

Greg Heath slid out of our booth and helped his employee pick up the tray and broken glass. He also paced the "splash zone" a few times before calling for someone else to bring a mop and broom.

"Aw, crap," I whined, "now I've gone and screwed things up with Greg."

Annabelle pulled me close to her in a half-hug. I laid my head on her shoulder, my hair spilling across her arm. I sighed and felt exhaustion catching up to me bit by bit.

Greg returned to our table, grim-faced. "I don't know what to believe, exactly, but some of the beer spilled around some pretty strange footprints over there, and something scratched up the floor there pretty bad. Like claws."

I sat up, heart in my throat. "So you believe me?"

Greg shook his head. "Not saying that, but I'll say there's more going on here than just your imagination."

An idea dawned on me. "Say Greg, do you suppose I could have a couple of bottles of that gruit?"

"What are you thinking?" asked Annabelle.

I held up a finger to her to see what Greg said.

"Well...I don't have much, but I could spare a couple. Why?"

"I doubt you'd believe me if I told you, but let's just say, it could help me a lot if a little of your special brew could do what normally takes enough to get me kind of impaired."

Greg shrugged. "Well, heather's known for mild psychotropic properties, so you could still be seeing things, but yeah, it does give a pretty good buzz. Sure. I'll go get you some for when you leave."

I opened my mouth to thank him, but was overcome by a yawn that made it more drawn out and less coherent. "Maybe we'd better go soon, it's been a long day and I've finally got a full tummy."

Annabelle patted me but looked at Greg. "I'll make sure she gets some rest."

Greg nodded and wandered off. I watched him go, among the trees and grass and rising moon, hearing coyotes howl off in the distance.... The ground shook with some kind of tremor, and I had to hold onto something solid, but the shaking continued. I heard someone calling in a soft, sweet voice. It was my name being called. I liked how the voice said it.

Something was patting my face and my eyes bumped open. I woke to see Annabelle staring at me for the second time today.

"Huh? What?" I said, disoriented.

"You fell asleep, love. Let's go."

"But we need the Heath Heather Stuff," I babbled, still half asleep.

She showed me a couple of bottles and a signed receipt. The dishes were gone, too.

Oh.

I let her stand me up and pull me along to the door. Night had fallen outside, and all the lights around the circle blazed, the towering Monument lit from all sides by spotlights.

"I'd take you home with me, but my truck's still up in Holliday Park," said Annabelle, looking around, uncertain of where to go now.

"S'okay, I've got a room downtown. That way," I pointed.

I don't recall getting there, but we got to my hotel, and I was even able to find my room key and recalled the room number without having to ask. I let us into the room and gave her the grand tour, pointing out my other clothes, which were all now dry.

Annabelle seemed nervous for some reason I couldn't understand, but I invited her to stay. She had some other questions and worries, too, but I kept nodding off.

I was too tired for modesty, so I slipped off my skirt, letting the Indians t-shirt serve as a nightgown. I felt like a magician as I removed my bra without taking off my shirt. I even gave her a flourish as I did it, saying "ta da!" as I dropped the bra on the floor.

I think she tucked me in, because that's the last I remember before falling into the bottomless well of sleep.

I lay on the forest floor, black silhouettes of trees waving their giant arms above me in a warm summer breeze. Night noises were all around me. I heard things rustling in the brush nearby. I heard night birds call as they darted from tree to tree. Or maybe it was the squeaks of bats.

I stood, feeling groggy and sluggish. Barefoot, wearing only a t-shirt and "oops" undies was no way to be dressed for these woods by myself at night.

I peered around, and saw light ahead, down the path I'd been laying. I padded along the path, my tender feet feeling every stone, and twig. Some of those stones felt like they might bruise, and I had to shift my weight from foot to foot to keep from falling more than once.

The light turned out to be a pool of moonlight in a small clearing. In the center was a pedestal with a sundial on it. Except now, I thought, it was a moondial. At the base of the moondial was an iron birdcage holding a small creature.

I knew deep down that it was my Minnie for real this time, and I ran toward her, heedless of the bricks and sharp quartz gravel that was the floor of the clearing. Something about the clearing, something odd...some kind of pattern, swirling and curving, but with straight lines too...it was familiar.

I felt like I'd broken a rule as I crossed, like I was getting away with something. I didn't care. Minnie'd come from me, and I needed her back. She'd been stolen, and that was wrong, much more wrong than breaking the rules of some game I couldn't recall.

The closer I got, the more I felt like I was trespassing, that unheard alarm bells rang somewhere nearby.

That someone watched me. Or some *thing.*

"I'll have you out of there in a minute, Minniekins!" I called to my tiny friend.

Minnie didn't reply out loud, but I could see her waving her hands across and back, warning me off.

No. No more games, I couldn't let anything stop me. I crouched before Minnie's cage and ignored her frantic, panicky motions for me to leave her imprisoned.

I pulled the latch on the cage and opened the door. It groaned and squeaked and snapped off in my hand, crumbling to rust dust.

A horn sounded in the near distance, not far down the trail I'd come from. Dogs barked and howled, and I heard the clatter of hooves.

I took my eyes off Minnie to turn to look. I couldn't believe what I saw. Queenie sat astride a giant horned stag, wearing the same horns I'd seen on her in my dream of the goblin market. She seemed to cast a terrible, unearthly light from her skin, and her eyes shone like red lanterns, beams of crimson sweeping ahead of her stag and pack of dogs, searching, searching....

Resting her gaze upon me, I felt a literal heat as she spied me. A sick, cruel smile spread across her alien face, and she smacked her mount with a loud crack of her crop.

I ran. I didn't decide to run, I just found myself bolting away from Minnie's cage, the pedestal and moondial, across more bands of the pattern and off on another trail.

Rocks punctured the bottoms of my bare feet, weeds and low branches tore at my legs and arms. I didn't care, I didn't think, I just fled.

The horn sounded again, and dogs bayed and hooves thudded behind me, all too close. My breath came in ragged gulps as I pushed myself past my limits, knowing now what it meant to run for my life.

Dogs nipped at my heels and I tripped, sprawling full out on the ground ahead of me. I tried to scramble to my feet, but several dogs piled up on me, biting my arms and legs. The pain would come later, all I felt now was shock and terror.

Queenie whistled and clapped and I heard her jump from her seat on the tall stag's back to the forest floor. The dogs' weight lifted from me and Queenie grabbed my hair and yanked me to a sitting position.

She put her face right up to mine. The light shining from her was blinding at this range, and her eyes were bright and hot.

"Challenge me, the Queen of the Hunt, will you, bitch? Well I shall give you the same choice I gave your man. Give yourself to me, body and soul. Serve me. Or I'll take your life right here and now and my dogs will feast on your flesh."

I didn't answer. I *couldn't* answer. I felt as though the wind was knocked out of me. I couldn't even whisper or cry out.

"Answer me!" screamed the fairy Queen, shaking me by the shoulders. My head lolled back and forth, her eye-beams seared my skin, her fingers froze me where they touched.

I still couldn't answer. What would I answer if I could?

Most terrifying of all, I didn't know the answer to the question.

She spat in my face, hissing.

The spittle felt cold and as it hit, I saw light, brighter than her skin and brighter than the near-full Moon. Yellow, warm light.

"Skye!" it was Annabelle's voice! She should flee...I couldn't bear it if Queenie captured her too!

"Run, Annabelle, run!" I cried out, now able to speak. But as I did, Queenie and the forest scene all dissolved into my hotel room.

Annabelle held me by the shoulders. An almost empty water glass lay on the bedsheets and my face, hair and t-shirt felt drenched with cold water.

"Oh! Oh!" It was all I could manage at first, I was so confused.

"You were having a nightmare, you cried out, then... Skye, you started to bleed from scratches in your arms. I freaked out and had to wake you up, I'm sorry..." Annabelle shook as she held me, leaning over me in bed.

I looked at my arms, feeling stupid. Sure enough, there were scratches and bite marks on my skin, though they faded as rapidly as my recollection of the details of the dream.

After a minute of breathing hard and wiping water from my face, all that was left were some fine pink lines.

And my blood on the bedsheets and my t-shirt.

I told Annabelle what I'd seen and felt and she listened without a word. Some people listen only with half an ear, more concerned about what they'll say next than what they're hearing at the moment. Annabelle only listened. I can't tell you how much it meant to me to be heard, understood, and believed.

I couldn't tell her, either, so I showed her. I pulled her into bed with me and wrapped myself around her, holding her with my whole body as I kissed her full on the lips.

She returned my kiss with a gentle passion, running her fingers through my hair and stroking my back. I found myself pulling at her clothing, but she pulled away and bit her lip.

"Did I do something wrong, Annabelle?"

She shook her head. "N-no, but I rush into things too much. I'm not too proud of some decisions I've made, following my heart or my dick."

I felt my eyes widen. "Oh my God, you have a...?"

She laughed and punched my shoulder in play. "No! Just an expression. But wow, you should see your face!" She laughed, and it was contagious, soon both of us were gasping for breath. One of us would manage to stop for a second, but the other would explode into a flurry of giggles. We laughed until we cried and then, laying in each other's arms, we caught our breath and looked each other in the eyes.

"Seriously," she said after a moment, "It's the best way I can describe it. I've let my body lead the way and it screws things up that could have been good."

I sighed. "And I guess maybe rushing into my first time with a girl isn't the best idea."

She raised an eyebrow. "Your first? Why Skye, I don't know what to say!"

I grinned. "You could say, 'yes'."

She stuck her tongue out at me and gave me a raspberry. "Tell you what, if you still feel that way on a day when we haven't both saved each others' lives a few times, I might just accept the honor."

We kissed again, since there didn't seem to be much else we could say. I felt sleep coming on again now that I'd calmed down, and from the tears of laughter. I felt safe and loved in her arms.

"Stay here in bed with me at least," I murmured as I nibbled her ear.

I felt her hesitate, then nod. "You know, it's funny, we don't even know each others' last names. Or very much about each other."

"Yeah, I know, meeting you this morning seems ages ago. Skye MacLeod, at your service, ma'am!"

She giggled. "You're kidding."

I sighed. "No, I'm serious, my parents think they're funny."

"I think it's an awesome name! Romantic, even."

I snorted. "I got a lot of teasing when I was a kid. I was taller than most other girls, so...Head-in-the-clouds, they called me, among other things. So my feelings about my name aren't so romantic."

"Hey, kids'll tease over any name. I'm Annabelle Adams. Just how many times a day do you think I heard the theme song to that TV show sung about me?"

I giggled. I couldn't help it. "Okay you've got me there. My parents spelled my name S-K-Y-E, but as a teenager I ran away and dropped the E on the end, to sort of own the taunts. After they died, I decided to go back to S-K-Y-E in their honor."

"Oh, I'm sorry," said Annabelle, hugging me close.

"No, I like it spelled this way, now. It feels right."

"No, not your name, I meant...."

"I know what you meant, hon. It's still not easy. We hadn't been on good terms, then there was the accident...I don't really want to go into it all, but it was so hard. Is so hard."

Annabelle was quiet for a bit, and I felt a bit like I'd thrown a bucket of cold water on the conversation.

"So anyway, funny thing about my name. There's this island off of Scotland called Skye, with an 'e' on the end, where Clan MacLeod lives. My parents never told me that. I found out when I got into genealogy after they died. I don't even know if my parents knew when they named me."

"See? I told you it's a cool name, with history and heritage all wrapped up in it," enthused Annabelle.

We lay there in silence together awhile, and then Annabelle turned out the light and curled up around me, hugging me to her. I heard her breathing slow as she fell to sleep. Sleep pulled at me, despite my whirling thoughts and worries. I hoped I'd have a non-paranormal dream this time. My last waking thoughts were of Annabelle and me dancing tomorrow night at the Danse Macabre.

When I woke, I didn't recall any dreams at all, and my aches had just about gone away. Annabelle wasn't in bed with me, so I got up and looked around. Not in the bathroom, either, so she'd left. I paced around a bit, deciding what to do next. The morning sunlight felt good as I walked to look out the window onto downtown Indy.

The door opened behind me as I stood there, and I turned to see Annabelle letting herself in, holding a platter with breakfast on it.

"Waffles! Oh Annabelle, you do love me!" I cried, grinning at her.

"You know it, babe! Along with the finest individually wrapped syrups and butters. Coffee too!"

We sat at the little desk next to each other, eating, looking at each other in the mirror. I thought we looked good together.

"So, I have a problem," said Annabelle after we'd finished eating.

"Huh?" I said.

She smiled at me. "Well, if we're going to a dance, I've got nothing here to wear. My truck's still up at Holliday Park, so running home to find something might be difficult."

"Oh, yeah. Well, my dress is at my friend Leslie's up in Broad Ripple. I could give him a call and see if he might have something for you to wear?"

Annabelle shrugged. "You think he's my size?"

I thought of little Annabelle superimposed over bear-like Leslie and laughed. "Oh! No no, not his clothes. He's a costumer for the game, he works absolute magic with clothes and makeup."

"Oh, okay. Sounds fun!"

I called Leslie and found him already up and busy. I let him know about Annabelle and he asked me to bring her to him, he'd see what he could do.

I announced that I needed a shower, and though I could see in her eyes that she was tempted, I couldn't talk her into joining me. Maybe I'd better slow down, I thought, remembering our talk last night.

The shower was amazing, and I have to admit I hogged it awhile. I couldn't see well when I got out, and I imagined the steam boiling out into the room as I came out with a towel wrapped around me.

Annabelle gave me a peck on the cheek as she passed, taking her turn in the shower. I dressed in my sink-washed olive skirt and matching t-shirt. She finished within only a couple of minutes, wearing the clothes she'd had on before.

We left the room and rode the elevator down. I visited the front desk and paid for another night. I used the special code for the Danse Macabre to get the discount. I'd chosen this hotel because I'd known about the deal, and because of its proximity to the canal walk where the Danse was to be held.

"Can we go get my truck before we go over to Leslie's," Annabelle asked me as we stepped outside. "Would it be safe?"

I frowned and shook my head. "No, not safe. But if it's important to you, we could see if King Bask can help us out?"

She shrugged. "I'd rather have it."

So we grabbed the next bus. George was driving, but his mood had improved, and he even smiled at us. Maybe it was because I wasn't yelling at the top of my lungs this time.

"I think that's yours," George said to Annabelle. "But please leave it there until you get off, okay?"

"Oh the poker!" she said. "I can't believe I left it on the bus yesterday."

We sat next to each other, the bus once again almost empty. "So, you magically appeared on a bus and you think forgetting the fireplace poker was the hard-to-believe part?" I nudged her and grinned. She stuck her tongue out at me.

I looked around the bus, but Bask was nowhere to be seen. Hmm.

"No Transit King?" Annabelle asked.

I shook my head. "Not that I can see. I've got some Heath brew in my purse, but I think I should save it for later."

She nodded. "What about in the park?"

I shrugged, enjoying my clearheaded morning too much to start drinking already. "We'll see what happens when we get there, I guess."

The bus rolled along, and we reached our stop without any sign of my diminutive benefactor and no evidence of other otherworldly agents. Annabelle remembered to pick up the fireplace poker before we stepped off at Holliday Park.

The bus sighed and rumbled away. I knew that it'd be another hour before another one came by. I watched the bus go, hoping this wasn't a stupid risk.

I turned as I heard Annabelle clear her throat. She held the poker up like a sword. I followed its point to see a wolf rounding a low wall at the park's entrance, teeth bared.

Chapter Ten

Annabelle put herself between the wolf and me. The wolf didn't back down, but didn't come closer, either. Instead, it sat back on its haunches like a begging dog. It blurred and I had to blink a few times, thinking something was wrong with my vision. In its place was a familiar figure.

I put a hand on Annabelle's arm. "It's okay, I think. That's Deke, he's okay."

Deke smiled. "You're lucky she put me on guard duty, and not one of the others. Still, you shouldn't be here, Skye."

"We just need to get to the parking lot and take my friend's truck," I explained. "Can you let us get in and out? I promise, we're not looking for trouble."

Deke thought about this for a bit and then said, "Maybe. First, any progress on our deal?"

I shook my head. "Nothing yet. Even if I did, I don't think it'd be safe to say anything here, do you?"

He shook his head. "Yeah, you're right. Go on in, I didn't see you. But watch yourselves, and don't stay long."

I took Annabelle's free hand and we walked as quickly as we could without breaking into a run, toward the parking lot. I felt exposed and blind. I thought about the potent beer in my purse. My gut told me I needed to hold off.

Still, I could swear I felt unseen eyes watching us pass. I shivered at the thought of being captured by the frogmen again, and at what Queenie might do this time. I remembered her terrible glowing face, her burning eyes from my all-too-real dream last night.

I thought about other times I'd seen things, out of the corner of my eye, and in reflections. I stopped Annabelle for a moment while I rummaged in my purse. I came out with a compact mirror and looked through it at various angles.

The fact that I didn't see any frogmen didn't reassure me very much. Sober, my second sight wasn't very reliable.

I kept the mirror out and glanced at it quite often as we made our way to Annabelle's elderly SUV. I'm not much for big vehicles, but the sheer size and rustiness said "big iron" to me. I hoped it looked like death on wheels to an iron-fearing fairy-worlder like Queen Howl and her minions.

Once we both got inside, Annabelle and I slammed and locked the doors. The heat of the closed truck was oppressive, as it'd been soaking up the summer sunlight all morning. Still, we left the windows up as Annabelle started the engine and turned on the vent fan full-blast.

"Sorry, no AC," she said, but I preferred sweltering to exposure. She backed up and pulled out of the lot.

I thought I caught a glimpse of something big and warty in the side mirror. When I looked right at the mirror, nothing was there. There was a clatter and I saw dents and scrapes appear on the side of the car.

"Froggies!" I cried, "Step on it, girl!"

Annabelle pushed the accelerator down, and the big truck's tires squealed on the pavement. I was pushed against the side door as we rounded a corner. She braked hard and swerved to avoid some pedestrians, and then I was thrown toward her as we turned the corner toward the park exit.

Standing in our path was a wolf. I couldn't tell if it was Deke or another one. Annabelle laid on the horn and the truck sped up. The wolf's hackles rose and it leaped at us.

I think I screamed. How embarrassing.

The big animal bounded off the hood and over the roof, and I saw it land on its feet behind us as we tore out of the park. Annabelle ignored the stop sign and we came inches from clipping the back bumper of a hatchback that was crossing the intersection as we escaped.

We both whooped with relief as she drove us down the road and away. I tried looking in the rear-view mirror using my peripheral vision in hopes of spotting pursuit, but I didn't catch anything.

I guided Annabelle to Leslie's place and he greeted us at the door with a black lace tutu in one hand.

"Annabelle, this is my dear friend Leslie. He's a cosplay wizard. Leslie, this is Annabelle the firefighter, she's the one who saved my life yesterday morning."

Leslie shook Annabelle's hand and favored her with a broad smile. "Thanks. I had a bad feeling about her going home from here that night. I'm glad she's found herself a guardian angel."

Annabelle smiled in reply, turning a little pink.

Leslie looked Annabelle up and down, and then showed us in. Annabelle was silent as she watched Leslie make his way through the explosion of clothing, fabric, accessories and big plastic storage bins in his living room. The room was hot and stuffy, but I found the clean laundry scent in the air calming.

Leslie wrapped the lace tutu around a dressmaker's dummy that already wore a black leather bodice, and I heard the ripping of Velcro as he adjusted the waistband a few times to fit.

Once he was done with that, he riffled through a clothing rack and came up with the hanger with my dress on it. Only he'd added more gold embroidery along the seams and hem.

I cheered and took the dress from him. He pointed at a couple of open bins. I picked through packages of pantyhose, fishnet stockings and socks. I decided it'd be too hot for any of those, fashion be damned. My legs'd do okay by themselves; they seem to be my most popular feature.

I picked a pair of golden strappy heels from another bin and headed to the bathroom to change. Leslie was already measuring a flustered-looking Annabelle. She met my eyes, and I winked at her as I shut the door.

I stripped off my skirt and t-shirt and had to unbutton the shoulder of the dress to wriggle my way into it. Leslie must have done more alterations to it, as it was a more snug fit, hugging me like a lover. The dress worked magic, giving me an actual waist, the fit of it showing off my boobs and bottom as well.

I buckled on the heels, and while I often worry about my height making me stand out too much, I thought it might be a psychological advantage to tower over Queenie when I ran into her at the Danse.

And Stuart couldn't ignore me looking this hot.

I turned around and around, looking at myself in the mirror for a long narcissistic few minutes.

Wow. I'd even do me.

I was startled by a knocking at the door. "Oh! I'll be right out!" I kicked my clothes into a corner and opened the door.

Someone was in the room with Leslie, someone I didn't recognize as Annabelle at first. She wore combat boots, fishnet stockings and a cute, short kilt skirt that had purple panels in the pleats. On top, she wore a black fitted t-shirt with a short black tuxedo jacket with tails. Her lips were done up in lipstick that matched the purple in her skirt.

"I'd have given her pants to go with the coat, but I don't have time to alter anything to fit," said Leslie.

"He means I'm too short, but he's too nice to say so," said Annabelle, putting one hand on a hip and posing for me. "So? What do you think?"

"Annabelle, you're a girl! Why didn't you tell me?" I said, putting fingers to my lips in mock surprise.

She scowled. "It's the skirt that gave me away? Damn."

"Hon, you're gorgeous, that's a really fun look!" It still felt strange, my attraction to another woman. "I like the contrast of feminine and masculine, skirt with tux."

She brightened. "Good. With you looking that sexy, I thought I'd let you be the girl. I tried to get Leslie to do me up as a guy, but he had other ideas. I guess this'll do. Thanks, dude!"

They didn't hug, like I thought they might, but Leslie looked pleased as he looked her over. They just nodded at each other.

Leslie sat me down and started painting my face. He had a mirror set up at the desk where I sat, so I could see what he was doing. He made my fair skin even paler. Candy apple lipstick and shiny lip gloss matched my red satin dress. A touch of blush to my cheeks made me look less like a mannequin and more like a living doll. He used mascara on me that made my lashes look long and dangerous somehow. A touch of eyeliner with dramatic curls past the side of my eyes added to the mysterious, exotic look. Leslie didn't bother painting my nails, but just glued on some wicked long and curved fake ones.

My favorite touch was his application of a serpentine dragon temporary tattoo, winding up and around one of my calves.

My only disappointment was the little gold purse he handed me. I hated to part with my voluminous bag, since it still held most of what I owned now.

I had to admit, the big black bag didn't go with my Danse outfit. I transferred as much as would fit in the dainty gold clutch purse. Worst, my Heath brew bottles wouldn't fit, not even one of them. I'd have to drink one before the Danse and hope it'd be enough.

I stood up and modeled for my date. Annabelle whistled and grinned. "Oh baby, I'm going to be the envy of everyone there, with you on my arm."

I felt myself blush under the makeup. "Actually, you'll sort of be on *my* arm, I'm kind of royalty there, you'll be my consort. And I think you'll get plenty of attention for being yourself."

"Consort, hmm? I can handle that. You'll protect me from all the big bad vampires?" she grinned.

I nodded, serious. "No one will dare touch you if you're there with me. There may be some who outrank me, but I've got a lot of influence in several courts. I'm not someone to mess with. Stuart will find that ditching me for Queenie will hurt his position quite a bit."

She laughed. "So, breakups in the real world affect the game?"

I nodded again. "It happens. Technically, we're married in the game, though not in real life, and that'll continue in name until one of us calls it off officially with the Night Duke. But no one really wants real life drama to spill over into the game, so I doubt it'll even come up at the Danse."

"It sounds complicated," said Annabelle, chuckling.

"Oh, it is. Being a pretend vampire can be a lot of work, it's not all biting people and acting sexy. There's all this intrigue, duels and backstabbing. It's a lot of fun, at least for us. I'm sure it seems strange...."

She held up a hand. "It's okay. I'll just follow your lead, and you can try to keep me out of trouble."

I smiled at her and stepped up to kiss her. Leslie stopped me. "No messing up your makeup. Not this early anyway. I should have matched your lipsticks better, hmm? We'd best get going anyway. Help me load up?"

I put my flat sandals back on to help Leslie by carrying a few crates to his van. After two trips, he made me stop. He said he disallowed sweating on my part, it was going to ruin my makeup. Meanwhile, Annabelle seemed to be ant-like in her ability to lift and carry heavy loads without breaking a sweat.

She's showing off for me, how sweet!

After loading Leslie's mobile costume shop, I hugged my large friend and we parted. I hopped into the passenger side of Annabelle's truck, and as soon as we buckled in, she followed after Leslie's van. He led us downtown, and since it was Saturday, we found free meter parking on a street overlooking the Canal. Perfect. Arriving this early had advantages.

Still, for something as big as the Danse Macabre, there was no underestimating how eager gamers could be about getting started. Leslie was just putting on the parking brake as some gamers I knew approached. Leslie smiled and bid us farewell so he could attend to transforming them into vampires with his costuming magic.

We'd missed the official beginning around four in the afternoon, but nightfall wouldn't be for hours yet. So as I got out of the truck, I was very aware of the full sunlight. As a vampire, the character I play should cringe, hide and take severe damage from being out in the daytime.

Annabelle seemed to read my thoughts. "Aren't you supposed to burst into flames or something?" She couldn't help smiling as she said it.

I mimicked surprise, glanced up at the sun and cringed, screeching, "Argh, I'm melting, melting! What a world!"

She laughed and pretended to shade me with her hands, held up over her head.

I quit the act and said, "Well, most vampires would have a serious problem with the sun, but I'm no ordinary vampire."

She tilted her head to one side, curious, listening.

"My character, Sofia, has been around awhile. I lost a bit of experience and power moving from the Chicago Duchy to Indy. But I'm still more powerful than most vampires. I work at it. And one of the things I'd worked on was building up a resistance to the sun's light. It's only possible for more powerful vampires. And in the game, I'm a really powerful vampire."

"Sofia, hmm? Should I have a vampire name?"

I nodded. "We'll have to think up something for you. Honestly, I think it'd be best for you to play one of my thralls, a human I've basically seduced to do my bidding."

She arched an eyebrow. "Really?"

Oh dear. "Well, it's not like it sounds. As my thrall, you'd be under my protection. If you came in as a newbie vamp, you'd be fresh meat, to be recruited, subdued or destroyed."

She folded her arms, thinking this over.

I brushed her elbow with the back of my hand, so as not to scratch her with my fake nails. "Don't take it so hard. If you want to play this game later, if we make it through, it'll be my honor to sire you."

"Do *what?*" she protested, eyes widening.

I laughed. "It's a path from thrall to vampire. We pretend that I bit you and turned you into one of the creatures of the night. You'll get great starting stats in game since I'm an awesome vamp to have as your sire."

She allowed a smile now, and relaxed her posture a bit. "But not today?"

I shook my head. "No, hon. If you were a new vamp, you'd have to hide indoors until complete darkness, and I need you with me. And as a human thrall, you're no more worried about the sun than a normal person."

She still seemed hesitant.

"Annabelle, I need you. I've lost my home, my boyfriend and a bit of my soul. Let me have this little bit of control okay?" I hated the quiver in my voice as I spoke. "Being a feared vampire noble is all I've got, even if it's imaginary. It still gets me some real respect among gamers anyway. Being my thrall is no small thing to these people, you'll have more influence than some vamps who've been at this for a year."

She hugged me and murmured, "I guess I won't have to act all that much, love."

I took her by the hand and led her to some steps that led down to the canal walk. The sun sparkled on the surface of the shallow water, and a nearby fountain provided a soothing background roar. I could already see other people in costume roaming among the normals. Many of the vampire types had parasols or umbrellas, though strictly speaking that shouldn't help very much.

As we walked along arm in arm, there were people who stared. Jealous, I'm sure. Annabelle seemed unconcerned, and while I might be uncertain other places, in the game I'm in my element.

"Ah, Lady Sofia, you look stunning tonight. Whatever is that confection you have on your arm? She looks quite... delicious," said a male voice from behind us.

I stopped walking but didn't look around. "And you will find yourself becoming dessert if you take so much as a nibble, Stein," I said in as cold a tone as I could manage.

Stein, though he was a Count, had only gotten that rank through appointment by the Night Duke as a favor, and everyone knew it. Implying threats on me, and those in my influence, was a sign of insecurity. The chip on his shoulder was showing.

Stein came around from behind to face us, bowing. He wore a black trenchcoat, despite the temperature being in the 80s, and sheltered under an enormous green plaid golf umbrella. He wore round sunglasses so dark that it was easy to see my Annabelle and me reflected in the glass. His goatee still had a ways to grow in yet. "Pray forgive me, Baroness, I meant only jest, and a compliment to your selection in...." He let the sentence trail off for me to explain in character what Annabelle was to me in the game.

"You may look at my consort, but you may not touch her," I said. I could sense Annabelle tensing up just a bit, and I could feel her looking at me. I just stared down Stein, controlling my expression.

"As you please, Lady Sofia. Shall I see the both of you at the Duke's address at sundown?"

I nodded. "Of course, I wouldn't miss it."

He smiled and moved on to mingle with other early arrivals.

"What was that all about?" asked Annabelle, with irritation plain in her tone.

I looked at her now, letting down my icy facade. "Lady Sofia isn't like me, she's haughty and doesn't take crap from people like Stein."

She shook her head. "No, I mean," she searched for words, then continued, "I mean, you didn't even introduce me, I felt like I wasn't even a *person.*"

I turned and let go her arm to take both of her hands in mine. I met her eyes with mine. "Look, Annabelle, this is just a game, and you're not used to it yet. I'm sorry this is a lousy introduction to my other world. But if I'd introduced you to Stein, that'd be acknowledging his challenge to me as an actual threat. I had to be aloof. It was Stein I was treating as less than worthy, not you."

She pursed her lips, and I wanted to kiss her so much right then, mingling lipstick colors be damned. She needed more reassuring.

"Besides," I continued, "you haven't told me your game name yet. I didn't want to presume to invent something. Or put you on the spot."

She relaxed a little, and asked, "Okay, I get it, I think. Who should I be?"

I shook my head. "No, that's up to you. If you want advice, I'd pick something descriptive, something to go with the personality you want to project in the game. But you should name yourself, love."

She nodded, smiling just a little around her eyes now. I think I passed a secret test. "Well, I want to be, well...if we're supposed to be someone different, then maybe I'll take a cue from my outfit and be an artist, like from Mass Ave, a bohemian type that got too caught up in the romantic vampire fantasy. You, being a rich, sexy vampire Baroness, commissioned work from me and got jealous of my other clients and had to make me yours. But I'm still being tamed, right?"

I grinned at her. "You catch on fast, that's good. So, what's your name?"

"Something French, maybe. I'm thinking of that hot tomboy exchange student from Better Off Dead? Monique! That's me." She let go my hands and twirled, making her skirts and tails fly out around her, grinning.

I hated to break my game demeanor, since the goal is to stay in character as much of the time as possible, but I clapped and let her swing me into an embrace, catching me off balance. Her face was an inch from mine, and if she let go, I'd hit the pavement. She almost kissed me, but instead she grinned and set me back upright.

"Untamed is right! Okay, I can work with that, my Monique."

That having been settled, we made our way along the path. We mingled with a few more folks, mostly thralls running messages for their sun-fearing masters and mistresses. The thralls were generally quite excited to be there, and seemed very impressed by our costumes. Annabelle enjoyed meeting other thralls, since it showed her that they felt valued in the game and had a good time.

Then I spotted Hannah. She wore a threadbare grayish Nickelback concert t-shirt over black skinny jeans. I thought she looked kind of odd wearing big black plush Ugg boots in the summer, but I gathered it was the style among high schoolers and even some college girls my age.

I wanted to talk to Hannah, to see if she had any information, both in-game and out. She was one of my lines to Queenie now, but as a thrall, I couldn't approach her myself.

"See that kid over there in the boots?" I whispered to Annabelle.

"Yeah, wow, that's a look."

"Do me a favor and introduce yourself and let her know that I'm here. I'd like to talk to her."

Annabelle nodded. I'd expected her to ask me why I couldn't do it myself. Since she didn't, I took it as a sign that she was beginning to get the hang of how things worked in the game.

She slipped her arm out of mine and flounced up to the teenager. *She's really getting into her role,* I thought. I watched them talk for a minute, and then as Hannah looked over in my direction, I caught her eye and held it.

Hannah shook her head and gestured, explaining something to Annabelle, looking a bit sad. Annabelle looked back at me for guidance. I gave her the slightest of shrugs. I looked around to see if anyone was watching this whole thing, but if anyone was interested, they were being discreet.

After a bit more conversation, Hannah left Annabelle standing there and climbed up a set of stairs to leave the canal walk. Annabelle returned to me and sighed. "She says it wouldn't be a good idea to be seen talking to you. She says she still belongs to Queenie in the game, though she's working on changing that status as soon as she can. Queenie hasn't gotten here yet, as far as Hannah can tell. She says she'd ask to join you, but she's afraid of starting a fight between the two of you and being a pawn in that fight."

I nodded. "I guess that makes sense. I can't imagine what she'll tell the game judges or whoever she petitions in character to free herself. I doubt they'd believe Queenie locked her in a dungeon."

"I barely believe it, and I've seen goblins and trolls with my own eyes now," said Annabelle.

Her own eyes. *Oh Crap!*

"I just realized I forgot to drink up before walking all this way. I guess we have time to go back.... Maybe we could find a way for you to carry a bottle or two for me?"

Annabelle held up a hand. "Why don't I run back while you go on? I'll figure something out and catch up. All this water has me feeling like I need to pee anyway."

"I don't know. Maybe we should go together, it'd be safer," I began.

She shook her head. "No, with you being all noble and famous in this crowd, we can't go two steps without someone stopping you to suck up or deliver messages. It'll be quicker this way."

I still didn't like it, but I could tell Annabelle still needed to feel a little more in control, so I relented. "Sure, but call or text if anything happens," I said, taking my phone out of the ridiculous little gold purse. We did a quick confirmation of each other's numbers, she gave me a quick hug and air kiss and she was off.

Maybe he was waiting for me to be alone, or maybe it was just my bad luck, but within a couple of minutes of Annabelle's departure, Stuart blocked my path. He showed up with a posse of half a dozen thralls of both sexes, some of them mine.

Stuart wore the same old top hat and sport coat over blue jeans and a plain white t-shirt. He smiled as he saw me, and there was no polite way for me to escape as he walked toward me.

Like it or not, I had to be polite if I wanted to play the game. I felt a mix of emotions. Anger welled up in me, remembering how cold he'd been after the fire. Also, I hated the little part of me that felt relief at seeing him. I knew I was being stupid. Stuart and I'd been together for years, he felt like home.

"And here's my lovely wife, I can call off the search," he said, in character. My stomach did twists as the thralls forced laughter at his comment.

"Good evening, Count Chocula," I joked, faking a Romanian accent and a cold smile at my "husband". His in-game name was Drake Shula, a lame play on Dracula that he'd stuck with despite years of teasing by me and others. Others tended to regret mocking him. I could get away with it.

The thralls tried to hold back genuine laughter, but I guessed that they didn't know who they feared offending more, him or me. They had to know about our out-of-game split by now, didn't they?

"Ha, very funny, Sofia," he said, and may as well have slapped my face right there. It would have been a lesser insult to "forgetting" to use my honorific. Even as my in-game spouse, everyone expected him to follow etiquette. The thralls fell silent now.

"What do you want, my Lord?" I said with emphasis on the impersonal honorific.

"Why, I thought you'd need this," he said, handing me an index card.

"What's this?"

"It's your dance card. And I've taken the liberty of putting my name on as your first dance of the evening. I'll see you after the Night Duke's address, my love!"

Chapter Eleven

I almost tore up the dance card right in front of him. My real world gooshy feelings for Stuart took a back seat to anger and irritation at his attitude. But in-game, I had to keep my cool or he'd get the better of me. *Plus, I have to remember my mission. Someone's got to take Queenie down for what she's done to Stuart and the others. Someone like me.*

Something bothered me about this big show he was putting on. Why? Most out-of-game splits ended with the players' characters avoiding each other to minimize in-game drama. Stuart had been a good boyfriend to me up until the day of the fire. Yesterday. Why rub it in by forcing contact? *Why be a dick about it?*

My insides churned, my brain warred with itself. So I fell back on role-playing. I heard myself say, "Very well, my Lord." I pretended that letting Sofia talk for me made it easier.

I sometimes envy Sofia. She's powerful, feared, and even well-liked among the courts. My "real" life, lately, sucked hard.

Except for Annabelle. She saved my life, and continued to save me from just giving up. Having her along as a new player let me see the game, the gamers, and even myself, through her fresh eyes.

I hoped she'd get back soon.

Stuart tipped his silly top hat and bid me another formal, courtly farewell.

That's when I noticed two things I wished I'd noticed before.

First, Stuart had an anachronism on him. Slung in a leather holster on his belt, I saw what looked at first like a toy light-saber. It had a silver shaft with big rectangular cut gems, all candy colored, decorating the top and bottom of the hilt.

Shit.

Queenie trusted Stuart to carry the sceptre King Bask wanted, and I'd missed a chance to take it from him. I could have asked about it, or maybe even faked a hug and stolen it from him.

Though imagining myself running from Stuart and his six thralls in these heels made me laugh out loud. I'll need a plan to get it away from him and to the Transit King.

As if I didn't have enough to worry about at the Danse already.

Oh, and the other thing I noticed? Stuart had two shadows. And one of them was *mine.* I could see its arms waving in distress, as though being dragged behind him.

I started to follow Stuart, but was stopped short by a hand on my shoulder. I shrugged it off and said, "Not now, I'm sorry," but a nasal voice from behind me sent a chill up my spine.

"I beg your pardon, Lady Sofia, but it is important to me that I speak with you," said the Night Duke from behind me.

I froze, watching Stuart and his retinue sweep along the side of the canal, further and further from me. I sighed and turned and did a curtsy for him. "My apologies, Your Grace, I meant no insult."

Duke Ernest, the Night Duke, isn't short, he's as tall as me. He's not weak, I've felt those hands grip mine, and I wouldn't want to arm-wrestle him. But the Night Duke is skinny. Very skinny. From his protruding Adam's apple to his lanky frame to the ribs I could see exposed on his unbuttoned shirt, he gave the impression of being a recent concentration camp survivor. I'd seen the man eat not one but two Grand Slams at Denny's after a late night game. Everyone joked that he had the metabolism of a nervous little dog.

He smiled. Everyone knows that the Night Duke, outside of the vampire game, is a master of military strategy games. There's an expression in those circles that Stuart's told me. If your opponent smiles, it's already too late. My feet turned to ice within my sparkly high heeled shoes, despite the hot, humid Indiana evening.

"Baroness, I wish to express my...," he paused, wetting his lips with the tip of his tongue. "I wish to express my *sympathy* for a certain *situation* in the realm of the mortal men," he continued, his voice measured and careful as a trial lawyer.

Ah. It was his round-about way of saying he knew about the out-of-game issues between Stuart and myself. Why would he care about that?

His eyes roamed up and down my body, taking in my face, boobs, legs and back up again. "It concerns me that these issues could effect our long-awaited Danse Macabre. I've spoken with your husband, and he has petitioned for a divorce, just a few minutes ago, and I have granted it." His tone was still as warm and friendly as a tax audit.

Divorce? Damn, that hurt. Stupid Skye...do you want to be married in-game to someone whose indiscretion has cost him his very soul? To someone who belongs quite literally to another? *To that bitch, Queenie?*

I felt proud as I managed to affect an indifferent air, "Yes, I expected as much."

"And while our court only requires one party to dissolve a union, the parting of such a high-ranking couple can not help but have repercussions. I wish to make you an offer," he stated, and I had to keep a groan silent by an act of will.

Maybe if I don't ask what the offer is, he'll reconsider, I thought with less hope than I had of ice-skating away from him across the canal.

He smiled again. "Since you are now available, I would like to have the honor of your hand in marriage this Midsummer Night, to be announced during my address."

The chill in my feet spread up my legs to freeze the rest of my body with horror. No! Sure, it's only in-game, but marriage to this weasel of a man? I mean, I didn't have anything personal against the man, but I had this vibe from him that he wanted me as a trophy, and to consolidate power, in-game. But the way his eyes roamed all over me, I felt sure he wanted the fringe benefits of touching me and hoped for more.

He must have read my expression as the horror rose inside me, because he pointed one finger to the sky. That indicated an out-of-character statement.

"If you're thinking of saying no, Skye, we'll have to throw chops for it, as I'm putting my supernatural charm power into it."

Now I did groan out loud. He wasn't the Night Duke for nothing. King Bask's words came back to me, "Anyone can be a King if they can defend the title".

I held up a fist, readying myself for rock-paper-scissors. He followed suit, grinning.

I figured him for a Paper kind of guy, so after the count of three, I threw Scissors. So did he. First round a draw. If I didn't win enough in a row, he'd overwhelm me with sheer skill numbers.

We threw again. This time I figured he'd switch it up to Rock, since it's more masculine, so I went for Paper. He threw Scissors again, winning the second round.

Shit!

I had to win this. I didn't want to be forced into a political marriage-with-benefits. It'd ruin the game for me, and it'd complicate my chances of repaying King Bask's favor. Not to mention my promise to try to free Stuart and Deke from Queenie. And save Minnie.

But most of all, I wouldn't get to spend as much time with Annabelle, I'd be up to my earrings in political intrigue, and wouldn't be able to leave Duke Ernest's side for the duration of the Danse.

One more loss and I'd be forced to say yes to his proposal, and there'd be no way out. I decided to do this on my own terms. I held a finger up in the air and said, out-of-character, "Look, Ernie, if you want this so bad, I'll say yes...on one condition."

He put down his hands, suspending the contest to hear me out. He put a finger in the air. "Yeah? What's the condition?"

"I've got a date with me, and she's a newbie, and the game has already confused her enough. If we get married for political purposes, I get to openly keep her as my consort, and I get my freedom to mingle in the Danse."

The Night Duke considered a moment, and then nodded. "Sure, that works." He put down his finger and said in-game, "What is your answer, Lady Sofia?"

I drew a breath. "It would be an honor, Lord." Ewww.

He smiled. "Excellent! Shall we seal this with a kiss?"

I raised a finger. "Not on your life, Ernie. You don't want me going around saying you're abusing your power in-game, do you?"

He raised a finger. "Pretend kiss, then?" His smile was gone, and his eyes pleaded.

I lowered my finger and studied him a moment, then put my hand over his mouth and kissed the back of my hand. I rubbed at the crimson lip-print with the palm of my other hand and took a step back from him.

The Night King lost his cool composure and grinned like a little boy at Christmas.

"What the hell!" Annabelle's voice came shouting from a distance behind me. I spun around and saw her running up, carrying my big purse over one shoulder, a long scabbard on a belt around her waist.

Her face reddened, and her eyes narrowed. By the time she reached us, the Night King had left my side and was striding with arrogant purpose, brushing off anyone who approached him.

"Annabelle, it was a fake kiss, in-game. Look, lipstick on the back of my hand!"

She stomped one of her boots, angry tears welling up in her eyes. "I don't have any real claim on you, and I don't get this game, but I thought we had something special going on."

I put a hand on her shoulder and shook my head. "It's not like that. He's the highest ranking, most powerful character in the game. He just proposed marriage to me since Stuart's character is divorcing me, effective immediately."

"So you told him to piss off, right?"

I looked at her feet as I answered. "No. He was going to make me say yes, using in-game powers. So I said yes, on the condition I could keep you and wouldn't have to hang out with him for the rest of the Danse. He's going to announce our engagement at sunset, and I guess there'll be a short ceremony later."

I didn't look up. I didn't want to face her anger. She said, "This is bullshit, Skye. I'm not normally the jealous type, but I came here to be with you, even if I have to play your little slave girl. It could even be fun, maybe, I thought. I don't want to be here if I gotta be a damn nobody and get treated like it, too."

I looked up at her now. "Annabelle, that's just it. It is all bullshit. It's a game, with pretend marriages and pretend wars and pretend royalty. I won't ask you to ever show up for another game if you don't want to, but I need a friend to have my back tonight. I need you, Annabelle. Queenie's gonna be here, and she's shown she's got enough of a problem with me to steal my boyfriend, burn down my house and keep Minnie from me. We're in a game, but her game is a lot more serious."

"Well, then why don't we get out of these clothes and get the hell out of here? We can take my truck back to my place and hide out. You don't need this game, you don't need a phony baloney marriage, and you sure as hell don't need to screw around with Queenie."

I blinked back tears of my own. "Annabelle, I do have to be here. I made a promise to Bask, and since his token saved your life, I intend to make good on it. Stuart's become an ass, but he doesn't deserve to be enslaved by Queenie, and neither does Deke, or any of her other minions, for that matter. It's like she's some supernatural freak who can't tell the difference between the game and real life."

Annabelle put my purse on the ground between us and looked at me a long moment. "Fine. I'll be there, but I gotta walk this off. I can't be there on your arm when he tells everyone you're gonna be his bride. I'll feel like a fool."

I tried to hug her, to comfort her, to make it all better, but she held up a hand. "Not now. I need time. Please, Skye."

Hot tears rolled down my cheeks. "Okay, love. Just please, come back to me. I need you. I really do. You don't know how much."

Her face softened for a second, and she wiped away one of my tears. White makeup came away with it. She started to say something else, but turned and walked toward a stairway to climb up and out of the canal walk.

I just watched her go.

After I calmed down a bit, I realized there were a few thralls hovering nearby.

Great, I just put on a show.

I put up a finger. "Give me a minute, okay? That wasn't in character. She's new."

They nodded and pretended to look elsewhere while I regained my composure.

Inside the silly little golden purse, I found a makeup repair kit Leslie'd left me. I blotted at the shiny trails left by my tears and dabbed at them with more white foundation. I smeared around some of the existing blush rather than trying to add more. I didn't want to end up looking like a clown. At least the mascara and eyeliner seemed waterproof.

Once my face was fixed, I opened my big purse and found the bottles of gruit and all my other stuff. I took out one of the bottles. Greg Heath swears by swing-top bottles for his private brews, so I was able to open it and seal it up again after taking a long drink.

The bitter, spicy, sweet gruit warmed my insides and the world changed around me. Shadows had already grown longer, so the other side of the canal was more full of vampires than this one. But to me, after my drink, the sky changed to a deep blue and I saw the stars. Auras burned their colorful glow around all the people I could see.

Oh yeah, the thralls still waited on me.

I signaled that I was ready to play the game again, and the thralls approached. They were a few of my own, I realized. Some other newbies I'd taken under my wing last session. They needed me to take them to the fountain circle for the address, unless they wanted to be challenged by the other vampires. They might have gotten away with it, but it'd be best not to take chances early in the game if you're still learning.

I let them come with me and had one guy named Harper carry my big purse. He looked a bit uncomfortable at this. I asked if he'd rather have his freedom to go by himself, and while he whined a bit and looked at one of the others, a girl, as if I should pick someone else, he agreed.

I patted the poor thing on the head, making him flush. Sometimes it's good to make boys uncomfortable. God knows I needed to feel a little bit in control at that moment. I'd make it worth his while in the game another day, if he did a good job.

"Let's go, sunset is nearing, and I dare not miss the Duke's address," I said, putting on a cloak of confidence I didn't feel. My thralls followed, and since no one else wanted to be late, I had no further interruptions along the way.

The circle held more vampires than I'd ever seen in one place, even more than back in Chicago. This promised to be a bigger event than anyone imagined when it'd been announced. I could see some real world vendors had set up carts to sell soft drinks, ice cream, hot dogs, and even tacos. One cart owner was clever enough to offer novelties like glowing bracelets and shiny bead necklaces, as well as plastic vampire teeth and tubes of fake blood.

The middle of the curve held a riser with a few mic stands and public address speakers. To one side was a table with blood-red punch and little paper cups, being filled by low ranking vampires and thralls. On the other was a registration table and information booth. This was where the in-game judges would settle disputes and note changes in official status. I nodded at one of the judges, Melanie, who smiled at me and pointed at a list where she made a show of signing me in so I wouldn't have to. I gave her the thumbs-up in thanks, out-of-character.

I spotted many of the higher-ranking vampires, and as the setting's sun shadow now covered both sides of the canal, the rest of the children of the night came out to party as well. I felt at home all of a sudden, despite all else that had happened, I was among my people. They might be a strange collection of misfits, weirdos and posers, but I loved them anyway. This shared experience created an actual little world, alongside the real one in which we all had more mundane lives. Here, we could all feel special and live out a fantasy not available in real life.

As I watched, individual auras mingled, forming a sort of collective purplish blue aura around the assembled vampire gamer crowd. But the pleasant dim aura had a feeling of corruption, taking on a redder tinge to one edge. The center of that corruption moved toward the stage at a brisk pace.

I watched for a parting in the crowd so I could see, but dread weighed down my stomach; I knew already who it'd be.

Her aura burning like a mobile bonfire, Queen Howl strode toward me. The crowd parted as she came. She wore the same purple velvet gown she'd worn at her castle, coldly beautiful and dangerous as she had there. The stag horns on her head shimmered as outlines in her aura this time. A posse of thralls and subservient vampires attended her. Their auras all contained a red tinge, and gauzy glowing tendrils linked each one of them to Queenie. *Like an astral umbilical cord, maybe. Or a psychic leash.*

The bitch wore my memory chip pendant around her neck.

I stood my ground, kept my game face on, and pretended not to notice her. I thought I could feel the heat from her aura, or else from her gaze, as in the dream, as she neared me. My thralls fell back behind me, though I was pleased that my purse-holder stayed at my elbow. I admired his courage.

"You never answered my question," Queen Howl purred as she drew within a few feet of me.

A chill went up my spine. So, it hadn't been a dream at all. Or not just a dream.

As Baroness Sofia, I gave her a cool raise of my eyebrow. "Lady Queenie, so delightful to see you at the Danse, I feared you might not be able to summon the courage. Bravo to you," I said. I wished Annabelle and Minnie were here to back me up. "I can't say I'd blame you if you'd stayed home."

I knew deep down that this was a terrible risk.

It was as though I'd thrown gasoline on Queenie's aura. Her thralls backed away a step, but to my amazement, no one else reacted.

She narrowed her gaze to a lethal intensity. "How... how dare you! I own these people, why should I be afraid to show up? It is you who should fear for yourself, for your very soul, child!"

I decided to hold fast. Despite the cold fear freezing my insides, I laughed at her.

There was a murmur around us as lesser vampires whispered among themselves. Good. *Let's put on a show, shall we, bitch?*

Queenie's eyes widened. "I could strike you dead right here," she said with a hiss.

I raised my fist, ready to throw rock-paper-scissors. I met her glare and said, "Are you challenging me to a duel, right here at the Night Duke's party, the Danse Macabre? I fear not only would I win, but you'd be disgraced for making a scene. Perhaps you'd like to reconsider?"

It was a bluff. I *would* win, in-game. Only a handful of vampires could threaten me one-on-one, other than the Night Duke himself, and they'd be risking a lot to do so. Queenie had gone up in level fast, but she was outclassed in my make-believe world.

Now Queenie laughed.

I raised a finger and leaned in close. I tried to make my voice low and dangerous. "I know you're not playing the same game as everyone else here, Queenie. But I do know that this game is key to whatever you're doing, and messing with me right here and now would ruin all that."

I put down my finger and said loud enough to be heard by others around us, "So what was it you said?"

Queenie seethed. Her aura shifted to a deeper red, dark and dangerous. I saw sparks crackle at her fingertips, as in my first dream of her. I started to doubt the risk I'd taken, she might just call my bluff and kill me right in front of everyone.

Just as she drew breath and raised her hands to threaten me, there was a terrible squeal, and everyone put their hands to their ears.

It was Annabelle. She stood up on stage, tapping the mic, which caused painful feedback issue from the big speakers. "Check, check," she said with a sweet smile and a wink to me.

How had she gotten up there? I owed that girl a kiss she'd never forget later. I blew her one in promise, almost forgetting Queenie next to me.

"It is my honor as a newly blooded thrall to introduce His Grace, Ernest the Night Duke of Indianapolis!" she cried, swiveling her hips to make her pleats swing back and forth. She took a step back. Trumpets played from the speakers as the Night Duke took the stage.

He lost the stoop I'd seen him with last, drawing himself up to his full height, which I revised to be taller than me after all. Annabelle was like a doll in comparison, behind and to one side. She kept her eyes straight forward as he addressed the crowd.

"Greetings! I see many friends here. I am glad you could all make it to my Danse Macabre!"

The crowd replied with applause and cheers.

He continued, "Much blood has been spilled this year, which is good." There was scattered polite laughter at this. "There is also," he said, indicating Annabelle and the thralls at the punch table, "much new blood in our ranks. This is also good!" Applause this time.

"Some fortunes have been made," he said with a nod toward Queenie. She still looked pissed, but she nodded back at the Duke all the same. "And some have been lost," he said, not singling anyone out for embarrassment.

"But tonight, I have the great fortune to make an announcement. Will the Baroness Sofia please join me up here?"

There was a murmur that rippled outward through the crowd as I brushed past Queenie toward the steps of the stage.

Oh boy, here we go.

I stepped up and into the stage lights. Annabelle broke her forward stare for just a fraction of a second to flick her eyes to meet mine. *Is that a smile for me, or is she just squinting into the lights?*

The Duke reached out his hand. I took it and stood beside him, facing the hundreds of vampires and thralls in the crowd, faces all turned toward us.

"Though I regret to announce the dissolution of the marriage of Count Shula and Baroness Sofia, one man's loss is my gain, as I like to say." He left time for some to chuckle. "I have asked Sofia to be my bride, and she has accepted! The ritual will be performed at midnight, and I will be pleased to have everyone here in attendance."

The crowd roared with applause, cheers and whistles. I was glad for the opaque white makeup, because I was sure I was as red as Queenie's aura at the moment.

Speaking of Her Bitchiness, she stood in the same spot, staring daggers at me. I offered her a saccharine smile that I knew she'd try to make me regret later.

I was wrong. She made me regret it right away. She snapped her fingers, and Stuart came out of the crowd to stand at her side. She shook her head and pointed, and he knelt before her. She stroked his hair like a pet, her eyes never leaving mine. Then she dismissed him with another snap of her fingers. He retreated back into the darkness.

I felt so conflicted. My love stood behind me as a thrall, my gross new fiancé held my hand for everyone to see, and my ex was being ordered around by a woman who seemed to want me dead.

What's a girl to do?

"And now," proclaimed the Night Duke, "let the Danse Macabre begin!"

Chapter Twelve

Music played at the Night Duke's command. The speakers shuddered with a rapid thudding of industrial electronica. Before I had a chance to think, the Night Duke grabbed my hands and whirled me into his bony embrace, then twirled me back out again. Incomprehensible electronic voices murmured and babbled to the beat. My new in-game fiancée jerked and stomped his feet, he swung and spun me around like a doll, even though I'm sure I outweighed him.

I watched the lights and people spin around me. The Night Duke cavorted always near me, rarely letting go of my hands. I caught glimpses of Annabelle, still on stage with the two of us, dancing alone, smiling and watching me.

I timed it just right, and the next time the Duke spun me outward, I held my ground and reached out to Annabelle, who hesitated only a heartbeat before grabbing my free hand. She spun to wrap my arm around her, and then held a hand out to the Duke.

I saw his face go through rapid changes, from irritation to confusion, but as my girlfriend took his hand, his face lit up. What a win for him to be dancing with two hotties on stage, how could he object?

We took turns dancing two and three at a time, even dancing all separate in a triad of sorts. I yearned to talk with Annabelle, to find out how she'd gotten up here, and to thank her for coming back. The pounding music and the hundreds of eyes watching the three of us made this impossible.

Stuart didn't get his first dance after all.

A blurry sea of motion out there in the darkness beyond the stage marked the crowd. The only individual presence I could pick out was Queenie, her powerful aura broadcasted her location.

The first song ended, and unexpected energy charged my body. I wanted to go again, but the Duke leaped from the stage. I watched in amazement as he walked up to Queenie and offered a hand to her. Unsmiling, she took his hand and stared up at him with dangerous cinders for eyes.

The second song began, an angsty, angry female lead singer screamed her heart out to Ska-like speed guitar beat. Hard to dance to, but people tried, bouncing around like popcorn. I took that opportunity to take hold of Annabelle's hand and led us both down the steps and into the dark of the Danse crowd. It took some careful dodging to keep from being stepped on or bumped into by the frenetic dancing vampires.

We ended up close to the edge of the circular pool at the end of the canal. Annabelle and I did our hyperactive dance, and I felt a sort of electricity in the air, feeding off the crowd around us. I smiled at her, and she smiled back at me. The dance should be tiring me out, I thought, but the quirky up-tempo beat and the emotion of the singer kept my feet and body moving.

"How'd you get up there?!" I cried to her over the music.

"What!?!" she said, cupping one hand to her ear.

I danced closer and slower, so as not to bang into her on accident, defying the driving rhythm of the song. *Faster, faster!* it seemed to scream to me.

I repeated my question into her cupped hand and ear, as loud as I dared.

"Oh!" she yelled. "Your new guy sent for me! He's got spies! He offered me honorary squire-dom!"

Wow. A squire on her first day?

This would piss off a lot of people if it got out. Years ago, when I first started playing, I'd had to play as Stuart's thrall for months. My girl had a ticket to nobility even before being turned undead.

Good move, Ernie. I grinned at Annabelle.

The song concluded with the singer's long drawn out scream. The beat slowed bit by bit to the thudding of a heartbeat. The heartbeat turned into a screech of a heart monitor marking the end of someone's life, mingling with her scream. Both cut off at once, and everyone just stopped.

People all around us cheered and clapped.

Then the music changed to something slower and far older... no one here had been born when this song had come out. There was laughter, cheers and boos as we recognized Barry Manilow.

Mandy.

I had to laugh and clap. What a terrible clash with the goth sounds! What could they be thinking?

Oh right. That Angel episode where the vampire with a soul sang karaoke. This had to be someone's iPod playing.

Just then, Stuart appeared, his face clouded with bottled rage. In a controlled voice, he asked Annabelle, "Excuse me, may I cut in?"

Annabelle pursed her lips and put her hands on her hips and drew breath, maybe to give him hell, maybe to spit on him.

I didn't let her.

"It's okay, my Monique," I said, using her game name. She stared at me, mouth open. I pulled the dance card from my purse. "He asked earlier. Just this dance, okay?"

She stomped a boot again, which I'm sure I'd have thought cute if I wasn't worried about her feelings just then. I added, "Trust me, I have my reasons. I'm all yours right after Barry's done."

Annabelle folded her arms across her chest and sighed. She flicked a hand to dismiss us, face stony.

I gave my hand to Stuart as the words, "I need you today, Oh Mandy..." echoed around the ring of dancers. He put his arms around my waist, and I put mine around his neck. Being over a head taller than my ex, he had to look up at me so as not to bury his face in my breasts.

Pain filled his eyes as we swayed to the old song. I felt it too, the all too easy feel of being together. But I saw something he didn't, the red aura of Queenie tainted him. The wisp of a thread that trailed off toward her.

"I'm so sorry, Skye," he began. It was a good start, and it made it so much harder to hate him. *Damn him.*

I shrugged, being as cool on the outside as I could. "I guess you didn't have much choice," I said, not believing it.

He shook his head. "I was tricked, I got lured by her out of the Starbucks and into a forest. Her wolves hunted me down and tore my skin, Skye. I'd have died out there if I hadn't taken her offer."

I bit my lip and looked off to one side. I didn't want to meet his eyes. I didn't want to feel sorry for him. *Just by following her, that was the real decision he'd made to betray me.*

"Like I said, not much choice. I'm sorry it had to end like that," I said, daring a glance back at his sad face. "We used to be so good together."

He nodded. "I know, I've been a lousy boyfriend lately...."

"Look, I could complain about your porn collection, your webcam addiction, I could gripe about being a World of Warcraft widow. I could spend time bitching at you for blaming the fire on me. But we only have this song to say goodbye. And if you really want to help, you can, you know."

He blinked. "How?"

"That baton on your belt, the sceptre. I need it."

"Oh, I can't. I shouldn't even have it near you, really. She didn't think you'd know what it's for though, it's kind of a twisted joke of hers."

I pulled us closer together, my hands behind his head as I lowered mine, my lips an inch from his. "You could say you were distracted by one last kiss, Stuart," I offered. His eyes widened and I could see him struggle. I can't recall the last time I was this much of a temptation to him.

I have to admit, I felt a rush because of the attention. I'd missed it.

"What is it, Stuart?" I asked, putting a thick dollop of syrup into my voice, hoping it sounded sexy and enticing.

"I...I can't."

"Tell me. Or let me take it."

He struggled, then said, "If you take it, she'll kill me. She'll pull me to her and rip my throat out, Skye. Is it worth my life to you?"

That stopped me. I'd loved Stuart for years, despite our waning relationship. Hell, I loved him even at that moment, even after his betrayal. He just wasn't my Stewie anymore.

More to the point, I wasn't his Skye anymore.

"But you can tell me, and maybe that'll help me?" I paused. "Song's ending. Do you want to kiss me goodbye or just wave?"

He wanted that kiss, I could see it in his eyes, feel it in his breath as he struggled inside himself. "Fine," he said, casting his eyes downward a moment. When he looked back up, he said, "It's your heritage, Skye. It's the hilt of your family's Fairy Sword. That's why, if I wasn't under threat of death, I'd hand it to you right now. I will, too, if you can live with my death as a result."

Shock flooded through me. He'd *die* for me now? After blowing years together on some hot piece of ass that beckoned to him while I waited for my shift to end?

Or was it a bluff to keep me from taking it and risking disfavor from his mistress? *No. We'd been together long enough that he couldn't lie to me, not about something that big.* I believed he was offering his life to me.

So, I kissed him. I didn't just give him a little peck. As the last chorus of "Mandy" faded, I gave him a true kiss, to thank him for the time we'd been together, and a kiss to show him what he'd be missing.

I kind of got lost in that kiss myself, if I'm being honest.

But it had to end, and when it did, we both just took a step back and held hands, looking at each other with sad eyes.

Something hard and small and cold was between his left hand and my right. I looked a question at him. He just said, "Shhh. I can't give you that, but I can give you something else that's yours. Drink it, but not near *her*, okay?"

I nodded, feeling confused.

Then Stuart and I let go of each other, and he turned and walked away. Back the way the thread bound him to Queenie.

I wrapped the tiny object in my clenched fist and walked the other way. I brushed off a few offers to dance as the next song began. I needed to be away before I lost it.

I heard Annabelle's voice calling after me as I reached the outskirts of the crowd. As the first tears welled up despite my best efforts to hold them inside. "Skye!" she called, and in an irrational moment, I almost corrected her with my game name.

But that didn't matter at the moment. I didn't want her to see me cry, but I couldn't just walk away, either.

So I stopped. I felt her arms slip around my waist behind me, and I felt her head lean into the middle of my back. I started to shake with the effort of holding it in, and she slid around so her hands clasped in the small of my back. I leaned down to bury my face in her shoulder, heaving with sobs of the ending, feeling guilty for not celebrating the new beginning I had with her instead.

She just held me and stroked the satin of my dress, the heat of her hands soaking through to my skin beneath. I couldn't hear what she said over my own crying, but the words sounded soft and soothing.

I realized my white makeup was coming off on her dark tuxedo and I brushed at it with a hand, blubbering something incoherent.

"Stop. It's okay. I get it. You want him back. I won't stop you, Skye. Just don't ditch me, okay? I only just found you."

I pulled back to meet her eyes and shook my head. My hair flew around both our faces. "No! It's not like that. That was goodbye, Annabelle. It hurts, but he made his choice. And I told you already, I need you. If you still want me."

She didn't smile, but she stood on tiptoes to plant a soft kiss on my lips. "Of course I do. I don't want to imagine not having you," she said. As she spoke, I watched her lips. I could see my lipstick mingle with hers, purple and red.

Purple and red. Something clicked inside me. I hugged her to me, smooshing her cheek into my chest. She let out a strangled cry that dissolved into a giggle.

Still, when we parted, her eyes looked just a little haunted and wary.

I leaned in and kissed her again. "Honey, I have something I need to do. I need a drink, for one thing, and I need to clear my head if I'm going to face Queenie again tonight."

She nodded and took my hand and led me around the curve and onto the straight path of the sidewalk along the side of the canal. The moon rose over the buildings on the other side, and Annabelle cast a shadow once again.

And so did I! My own shadow waved at us from the concrete at our feet. Her outline was not the same as mine ought to be—she didn't have a dress on, and her silhouetted hair was pulled back. Her feet did not attach to the bottom of my feet, and didn't walk as I did, but drifted along like a ghost. Still, I know my own shadow when I see her.

I pointed. Annabelle jumped, and I had to grab her flailing arm as she teetered on the edge of the water. "Oh my God!" she cried. "Minnie's back?"

I led Annabelle a few steps away from the edge, and we stopped. I stared a few moments more then said, "I thought she might be. Look," I said, opening my fist at last. "Stuart's parting gift."

In my hand was a tiny clear bottle, made of cut crystal. The facets formed the shape of a heart, and it had a stopper of cork and white wax. The bottle contained an inky blue fluid, and I thought it looked quite pretty as the moonlight glinted off of its many surfaces.

"Skye, what is it?"

I shook my head, still staring at the crystal bottle and its contents. "All I can think of is a magic potion. But since I can see my shadow, I think Minnie's essence is trapped in there. He said to drink it."

"And you trust him?" asked Annabelle, her voice just a little shrill. "Skye, Queenie *owns* him. He left you in a burning building, for crying out loud! The best that I can say about that is, maybe she made him do it. Please tell me you're not going to do it, or so help me, I'll...."

I looked at her. "You'll what? Stop me? Look, you're right, honey, I had visual proof that he's leashed by Queenie. But she doesn't know him like I do. She may control him directly, if she gives him orders, but Stuart likes his wiggle room, and his conscience is okay with leaving things out. I swear, the man should have been a lawyer. Stuart does what he wants if he can get away with it."

"It's only wrong if you get caught?" asked Annabelle.

"Yeah, exactly. He loves the game, and I think it's a turn-on for him, the possibility of getting caught."

"Would he gamble his life on it?" she asked.

I hesitated, but remembered his offer. I nodded to her. "Yeah. For something that matters to him, he would."

"And you still matter?"

I looked back toward the Danse. I heard confused echoes of a hard driving beat backing an aching, keening female singer. I saw the silhouetted mass of people, heads bobbing and arms flailing on the edges. The aura I saw could be my imagination at this point as the swig of Heath's heather gruit wore off.

"I think I do, even if it's too late now."

I pulled the cork and held the bottle up in my fingers to let the light of the moon shine through the glass around the dark liquid. "Call it a leap of faith, if you want. Call 9-1-1 if I'm wrong. Here's to my health!"

Annabelle's hand darted toward mine, but she pulled it back before touching me. I saw her eyes glint with moonlight as she watched me. She bit her lower lip and waited.

I tilted my head back and tipped the half-ounce of liquid onto my tongue. For all the world, it smelled like Nyquil, but it tasted like a strong liquor made of blood and anise seed. Thin and burning on my tongue, it had a metallic tang and ran down my throat without needing to be swallowed.

The night closed in on me, my vision narrowed to a tunnel, hungry darkness gnawing at the edges of reality. I felt myself fall, I felt Annabelle's arms catch me. I heard the sound of her voice, as though from under water. I felt my bottom touch the still-warm ground. I felt as though the world grew larger and larger around me. Or maybe I shrank smaller and smaller. Annabelle's head floated like a cloud in the sky. Her mouth moved but only surreal noise reached my ears.

A unique sort of chill filled me, one that I could not forget. The scars of the demon's possession lit up my nerves with an icy fire for an awful moment. It passed, quenched by a warm numbness. I welcomed it.

And then I remembered to breathe, and I came back from wherever I'd been going. Sound rushed in to flood my ears, along with the pounding of my pulse.

"Oh Skye!"

"It's all right, love," I said, warmed by Annabelle's embrace, "I'll be okay now."

My vision cleared and I felt more or less normal-sized, though the world still sloshed in slow waves around me. I found that if I focused on Annabelle, things steadied quite a bit.

"Well, it's about time, you big freaking idiot!" came the scolding voice of Minnie. She stood on the tip of my knee, a near-transparent ghost-like figure. *I'll need to drink more to make her solid.* She wore what looked like low-cut scrubs, but made of fine linen. I giggled at her teeny tiny cleavage that her top revealed and at the way she shook her fist.

"You, my little dear," I said, as the fog cleared, "are a sight for sore eyes."

"What? Hey! I just kept your ass from hitting the pavement and you're making fun of my height?" said Annabelle, scowling.

"Huh?" I said, looking back at her.

"Need I remind you," said Minnie, "she can't hear me or see me, O brilliant one?"

"Cut me a break, I think I just about died," I said.

"Yeah, I know, but what the hell?" asked Annabelle, letting go as she sat down next to me, legs crossed.

"No, no. I was talking to Minnie!" I exclaimed, feeling about half a minute behind the conversation.

Minnie put her hands to her cheeks and mimicked Annabelle's voice, saying "Ohhh!" in unison with her.

"Stop that!"

"Stop what?"

"Tee hee!"

I closed my eyes and rubbed my face with my hands. There was a clink and tinkle as the bottle hit the concrete. I groaned and took a few breaths and peeked between my fingers.

No glass shards lay next to me; instead, a sparkling of glittery crystal flakes melted into the air like snowflakes in July.

Minnie said, "Okay, I'm back, but I'm beat. Call me if things get interesting."

I pulled my hands from my face and Annabelle leaned over to kiss me. "Are you sure you're okay?"

"Now *that's* interesting!" cried Minnie.

"I thought you were leaving?"

My mini-me grinned and vanished.

"What!"

"No, no! Not you! Sorry. The potion was Minnie's essence, and drinking it brought her back to me. She was being annoying, but she's gone now."

Annabelle drew back to look around. "So after all this, I still don't get to meet her? Hey, at least you have a regular shadow now. Wait, what's your shadow doing to mine? Hey! That's just wrong!"

I had to laugh as my shadow did unnatural things to hers. In fact, the more I laughed, the funnier it all was to me, even after Minnie cut out her pornographic shadow antics.

"I think maybe you're poisoned after all," said Annabelle, peering into my eyes as I struggled to stuff my laughter back inside.

I heard splashing, and a familiar voice called to us from the water. "Ladies, would ye care for a ride?"

My laughter stopped as we both looked over to see a gondola slide up to the canal's edge. Bask, the Transit King, leaned on the boat's pole. He wore a mime's black-and white striped shirt, black capri pants, and a tri-corner hat. His foil crown perched atop the hat at an angle.

He grinned and swept an arm to take in the gondola. "Did ye think I only did buses? All aboard!"

Chapter Thirteen

I looked at Annabelle, and she shrugged. I took Bask's offered hand and stepped into the punt. The boat wobbled as I stepped into it, and I nearly fell in the canal. My pretty golden high heels didn't help. Bask kept me from capsizing the long, narrow boat, surprising me with his strength. I guessed that a lower center of mass helped on a boat like this. I sat facing back toward him on the gondola's bench, and watched as Annabelle stepped on, refusing Bask's help. She smiled and patted my knee as she sat next to me. She cupped her hand and faced me as she stage-whispered, "I've done this before."

"Aye, looks like ye have at that!" enthused the Transit King as he leaned hard on the pole and pushed us out into the calm waters of the canal. The boat moved smooth and silent, and I had the strangest feeling of isolation. Sounds that had been carrying down the canyon of the canal walk now seemed distant and muffled. I was much more aware of the splash of the pole as Bask pushed us along.

"Ah, I've missed this. T'was long ago when the waterways were my Ways. Before the rails, before horseless carriages, buses and interstate highways, my domain lay upon the waters that connected place ta place. 'Transit King' indeed! T'were a grander thing to travel upon the waters, when canals moved folk and their wares. They make the finest of the Ways, the straight tracks that tis my duty to Ward."

"Straight tracks, I've heard of that," said Annabelle. "The magic fairy ways."

"Aye, that they are, lass. Don't say 'fairy' though, it offends in some circles. Me, I don't mind livin' in the memory of your people in those stories. They're but fables, the garbled telling of tales. Stories with meanin' and morals at the ending. Happily ever afters. Lies, of course, to make your folk look good. It's not always been so good. Ye rule yer own world, sure, but ever have we lived in the spirit ways, 'twixt and 'tween your world and the world of dreams."

"You sure talk a lot," I remarked, sounding nastier than I intended. So I added, "For a guy who set me on a task that makes me choose between the life of someone I loved and a promise to you."

Annabelle bit her lip and looked at Bask. Maybe I'd said too much. But what was the little guy going to do, anyway?

He laughed. "Aye. Ye have me word, lass, I did nae know that'd be the case. Shoulda guessed, maybe, but I thought she'd hide it, rather than set a choice to ya. Maybe she thinks if you took it, she could turn you to her side. I mean, if you did, you'd be her kind of person, wouldn't ya?"

I nodded, anger rising in me like bile. "So what's so important about this thing, what's Stuart mean when he says it's my heritage?"

We passed under a bridge. The moon's light made his face unreadable. "He said that, did he? Then the cat's outta the bag, and I may tell you more."

"Why don't you just tell me everything, if you want me to succeed at your little mission? Maybe you can tell me how to get the thing from him without Queenie shredding his soul?"

Annabelle came into light again as the boat passed from under the bridge. I found that she was staring at me. I smiled at her, and she flashed a smile in reply, but didn't say anything.

"I'm bound by rules I can nae explain at this time, lass. Queenie and I play a game of chess, and can nae act directly against each other. But she means ye and yer friends no good, as ye know. But ye don't know jes' how much trouble she intends this night. I need ta tell ye about yer past, now that Stuart's spilled that bit. Then I need ta tell ye about the future. All right, lass?"

I nodded. "If you think it'll help. Guess I'm just a pawn in all this?"

"I think ye'll see yer more involved than ye'd think. First, let's talk about yer heritage, Skye MacLeod. Yer family's from the isle that is yer namesake, so yer in with both feet as it were. Not only that, but there was once a mighty warrior woman in yer family. The isle was named for her, though your histories don't say so. And so ye are her namesake and her kin in a direct bloodline. Her name I'll keep quiet tonight, for despite me magics, sound travels on the water quite fast and well. She trained the greatest Celtic warriors of the day, whose names still live on in yer tales. She was mighty with a sword, and also mighty with magics. She had the Sight as well."

I interrupted him. "Wait. You mean this is hereditary? If that's so, how come I haven't always had it? Why'd it take being possessed? I mean, I've got friends who were possessed and survived who went through something similar, and they see ghosts."

"Ah. That explains the magics already woven about ye. I'd hoped ye'd worked that out on yer own. I dinna know the way it works, lass. Maybe it woke a dormant power when it opened yer eyes to other worlds? Yer wee friend, the one who's separate but part of ye? She's not the means of yer power, but she helps, livin' in the spirit world like one o' my people."

"Your people? She's not a fairy?"

"Now lass, I told ye about the F-word. It gets attention ye don't want, if nae else. She's nae one of us, no. She's as ye must guess, a piece o' you. So she's a human spirit in shadow. Yer power is its own thing. Unreliable, is it?"

I nodded. "I have to be buzzed to see much more than glimpses."

He laughed, and the humor reached his eyes. It occurred to me that I'd never see warmth like that from Queenie. "That makes some sense, lass. Yer great-great-greats used ta prove their manhood by drinking from a family horn. Tis more of yer heritage. Yer a MacLeod all right! I reckon ye've proved yer manhood by now."

I started to object, but he cut me off.

"Nae lass, don't be hung up on innies versus outies on me. Yer girlfriend'd agree, such things do nae matter at the heart of things. Yer warrior woman namesake, too. She of the Isle of Skye so long ago, she worked with weapons, magics and took one of my people as her lover. Tales tell different, histories get all confused and rewritten by yer folk. But t'was she who brought the Flag of my folk as a token of affection back from shadow. Tis a keepsake yer family reveres to even this day, though tis in rags now."

The Fairy Flag. Mom and Dad told stories about that, and showed me photos of it when they talked about family history. It'd been ragged even for the first picture taken of it in the 1920s. "So what's the sceptre, if it belongs to my family?"

"Did Stuart tell ye of it at all?"

"Yeah. He said it was a...f-word hilt," I said, catching myself this time.

He grinned. "Tis more than a hilt in the spirit realm. Tis a full sword, the blade lighter, sharper, and harder than any ever made in your own world. T'was magicked and forged by yer namesake, Skye. It was lost for ages, now Queenie's popped up with it."

"If it's so deadly, why flash it under my nose?"

"That's exactly it, isn't it? She's taunting ye. Daring ye to take it. She's full o' herself, that one. But to tell more, I'd have to tell about that chessboard between us, and a Knight such as yerself must fight even though I may not speak of the moves ahead. Do ye understand?"

I shook my head. "No. But I get enough. How do I stop her?"

He sighed and turned the boat around, going with the current now, back the way we'd come. "More that I can nae tell, more's the pity. But were I to break the rules, she could too. Ye'll have ta puzzle it out when the time comes. I can tell ye a tale that may help."

"Go on."

"Once upon a time, there was a prophecy, that one with the blood of both worlds, a MacLeod chieftain, would come about. It speaks of a Midsummer night, just like tonight, under a moon like this one. It says that the Hilted Sword shall come back into its family. And ere midnight, the one of the blood will strike down a mighty Unseelie foe, knocking the crown from upon her head."

"Seriously?" interjected Annabelle. "I get it. Fairies are real." she said, and King Bask winced. She went on, "And some of these bastards are really bad news. You're trying to tell Skye that she's part Tinker Bell and some ancient prophecy says she's a Chosen One? Take a second look. She had to look up her name on Google, she's no chieftain."

I felt grateful for breaking the spell of the fairy tale Bask had been weaving. I loved Annabelle's way of cutting through the crap. Bask, I felt, was far more trustworthy than Queenie, but I didn't know how much of his crap I should buy.

Bask grinned at Annabelle. "Now ye know how we feel about yer tales of our people. Tis hard ta see how such a thing could truly be, isn't it?" He looked back at me and said, "Decide for yerself if this is about you, Skye. Mebbe yer the one in the tale, or maybe ye have yer own tale that's not written."

Music began to echo from the buildings around us, its pulsing beat unmistakable as that of the Danse Macabre. I looked behind me in the direction Bask pushed the boat. I saw the mass of dancing vampires and the fountain at their center. We'd come back much faster than we'd gone up the canal.

Bask followed one side of the canal until we reached the start of the curve of the circular end and fountain area.

"I may not approach closer, as this part of the chessboard is her territory."

"Hers? It's our party, she's just a guest," I growled.

"Guests may take advantage of their hosts. They may drink more than their share, make a mess that the host must clean up, or perhaps worse things, lass. Ye have a taste of the worse, but yet don't know the worst. Yer promise to me is second to teachin' yer guest her manners, do ye get me?"

I met his eyes, and even without any alcohol in my system, I thought I could see him grow a bit, take on a dignity that he hadn't shown, a grimmer face behind those laugh lines.

He's got a lot riding on this. Maybe everything. It's more than a game, I thought. Red and purple came to me again, the mingling of my lipstick with Annabelle's, the mingling of Queenie's red aura and the overall purple aura of the vampire crowd.

My people.
Oh!

"Holy crap. I know what I have to do!"

Annabelle had climbed out of the boat, and she blinked down at me from the side of the canal, looking confused.

Bask grinned. "That's the spirit, lass! Now remember yer clan motto, mind ye. Get back to the party and make yer family proud!"

I held up a finger. "Just a sec. I have to get ready," I said, taking a bottle of Heath's heather gruit out of my bag.

He shook his head. "Nae lass, ye'll need yer wits about you."

I popped the swing-top and smelled the spiciness of the heather. "And I'll need to see what Queenie's up to."

"Then 'tis better ta sip rather than gulp. Be ye'll not need it, when the time comes. Ye'll see clear enough without it, if you are the one from the story."

I held the bottle to my mouth and the taste of the spicy brew touched my tongue. If he was right, it would be better to have the Sight without alcohol. And I could always take a swig of it later, if I needed it.

So, I capped the bottle and put it away.

I let Annabelle help me out of the gondola and up onto the side. I turned to thank Bask, but the little King and his boat were nowhere to be seen.

"Crap, he's gone," I said. Annabelle jumped, startled, when she looked.

"What do you have to do?" she asked after a moment, shaking her head as if to clear it.

"Will you be my maid of honor, Annabelle?"

"What? I guess. I mean, it's sweet of you to ask...."

"It's just in the game...."

"I know."

"You're not going to be giving me away, just standing up for me, okay?"

She nodded and kissed me. "Outside of the game though?"

"I'm all yours."

She smiled, shy all of a sudden. She looked over toward the Danse. "Still doesn't answer what you're planning."

"Guess it's my turn to be cryptic," I said, "but I don't want to be overheard."

I pointed with my chin toward the shadowy figure of Hannah, who lurked at the edge of the dancers, watching us.

Annabelle risked a glance, then said in a low voice, "Okay, gotcha. Trust no one."

"Just me. Can you, 'Belle?"

"Never doubted you, Skye."

"So what's with the sword?" I asked. "Is it real?"

She patted the scabbard on her hip and smiled. "No, but it's better. I grabbed the iron poker from my truck when I went back for the beer. It didn't go with the costume, so I asked Leslie, who was still doing makeup and stuff. He handed me this belt and sheath."

"Good. We'll probably need it. If we face things I can see but you can't, I might need you to hand it to me."

"I've got something else, too!" she said, looking around to see who was watching. She reached into my bag and pulled out some paper packets to show me. Fast food salt packets?

"What are those for?"

"So," she said, tucking some into my little gold purse, "Legend has it that the Tinks have a weakness. They're OCD. If you dump salt in front of them, they have to stop what they're doing and count each grain."

"Seriously?"

She shrugged. "No crazier than any of the rest of this. I had some in my glove compartment, so I figured it wouldn't hurt for each of us to have some to toss at Queenie and her goons."

I grinned and hugged her. "Okay, let's go find the Duke."

On our way back into the main throng of the Danse, I noticed a line at the punch table that hadn't been there before. I also found Leslie walking away from the table, carrying a paper plate with a few shot-sized cups full of what looked like blood.

He greeted us with a cheerful rumble. "Well, if it isn't Night Skye and Fire Gal!"

I curtsied and Annabelle bowed. "Hey Hagrid," I teased, "Are you giving up the seamstress gig to be a waiter now?"

He chuckled. "Naw, just helpin' out some noobs. The punch has been declared to be 'blood' and as such, gives some temporary bonuses in-game."

Annabelle said, "Hey, I'm a noob, can I have some?"

He handed her a little cup full of the red liquid. "Sure, I guess it's Hawaiian Punch with some extra flavoring and food coloring."

Annabelle thanked him and tossed it back like a shot.

He added, "Keep the sticker on the bottom of the cup to show your plus one if you need it. Skye, you want some?"

I took one of the cups and held it to my lips and sipped. Under the sweet fruity punch, it tasted of ginger and a hint of something more exotic. Juniper berries?

I peeled the little round red garage sale sticker off the bottom and stuck it on my shoulder. It just had "+1" written on it. I figured I could use any bonuses I could get.

Just then, the Night Duke arrived. He also had a +1 sticker affixed to his costume.

"Bonus," I said. I held up a finger to Annabelle and Leslie and left them for a moment to take Ernie's arm. "My Lord, I must beg a favor of you. I am not sure how late I may stay awake, it's been a hard couple of days, as you know. Could we move the wedding up so that it ends at midnight, rather than beginning then? We'll have more of a crowd that way too, considering curfew for some of the younger members."

He nodded. "Very well, Lady Sofia. If you are so eager to be joined to me, I can arrange that."

The Night Duke snapped his fingers, and one of his attendants melted out of the crowd. He gave some orders, and the attendant rushed off to make preparations.

"I'm glad you've come around on this, dear Sofia, I think you'll rather enjoy the perks of being my bride."

I sighed. "I feel certain that I will, so long as you honor our agreement, Duke Ernest."

He patted my arm. "Don't worry. All will be well."

I disengaged my arm from his. "Since I am only a free woman for a little while longer, I wish to have a last dance with my consort, if you please?"

He frowned, but nodded. "Sure. You will hear the announcement shortly. Please be ready." He bowed to me, and then swept off into the crowd.

I found Annabelle alone, looking a little lost. She brightened when I returned. "Leslie had to go help other noobs," she explained.

I took her arm and towed her away from the blood line and into the mass of the Danse itself. The song was slow and mournful; I thought it might be a remake of an old song by The Cure. I held her close, and we swayed to the music. I was happy just to not talk for a while, and it was good to have her close to me.

Then I noticed something. I could see auras around me, and I hadn't had a drink. I remembered seeing them even as we got off the boat, now that I thought about it. Maybe Bask was right, maybe I wouldn't need booze tonight.

I wanted the moment to go on forever, Annabelle and I in each other's arms, swaying among my gaming friends. But of course, it couldn't last. Queenie danced her way toward us, leading a sad-faced Stuart. I'll give her this, it wasn't just swaying, she danced actual steps, maybe a waltz. Stuart might as well have been a marionette, the way she moved him around.

"Lady Sofia, I see you haven't left after all. I'm happy you decided to face your fate like your family always has. What's a game without an opponent?"

Her aura extended to show horns, and I could see a wolf-shape to Stuart's aura as well. It made me sad, but I hoped to free him soon enough.

"What's that? I'm sorry, I can't hear you over the roar of your smugness," I snarked, adding, "...Lady."

Queenie laughed. Annabelle nudged me to move away from her, and we swayed and stepped around another couple. Queenie and Stuart followed.

"I'm sad for you," she said, "It will all be over before your wedding can take place, dear sweet Lady Sofia," she said with syrup in her tone.

The music stopped. I parted from Annabelle, but still held her hand. I waited.

"There has been a scheduling change," said a teenage girl up on the stage, standing on tiptoe to use the mic. "The wedding of the Night Duke and the Baroness Sofia will take place momentarily!"

Queenie frowned and let go of poor Stuart like a discarded toy. It took quite a lot not to let my own smugness show right then. She glanced from me to Annabelle and back. Except she didn't meet our eyes. Her gaze flicked to the the +1 stickers we wore.

"Hmm. I don't know what you're up to, but it won't save you," she said.

I smiled and said, "I'm sorry, but I have to go get married. I shall see you in the receiving line, I'm sure!"

Before Queenie could reply, I led Annabelle into the crowd and toward the stage. "I hope you'll be okay through this. It's necessary," I said.

"I'll be okay, but honestly, I can't wait for this game to be over," she said, dodging vampires that almost bumped into her.

I guess I was in too much of a hurry, because before we got to the stage, I tripped on someone on the ground. I landed like a sack of potatoes on what turned out to be Stein, who was curled up on the ground, holding his stomach.

Annabelle helped untangle me from him, then we both crouched near him. "Hey. Stein. What's wrong?"

"Ugh," he said, blinking at me. "Something I ate, I think."

"Should we call someone?"

He shook his head. "I'll be fine, just get me out of the crowd, okay?"

I took one of his arms, preparing to share dragging duty with Annabelle, but she just hoisted him up over a shoulder, despite being much smaller than him. I must have been gaping at her, because she grinned and grunted out, "Fireman's carry."

She got him over to one side of the stage, where the Night Duke stood, waiting for me. "Is something the matter?" he asked, and he broke character, expressing actual concern.

Annabelle shrugged after settling Stein. "Not sure. I'd guess he should probably get a ride home. If it gets worse, maybe-."

Stein protested. "No, I'll be okay. Get me a bucket in case I puke?"

Annabelle borrowed a trash bag from the blood punch table and handed it to him. "Look, don't be too proud to ask someone to get help, dude."

He nodded. "Yeah, I know."

I looked at Ernie. He frowned, and shrugged. "Shall we?"

"Yeah, let's do it."

The Night Duke grinned.

"Not that. Cut that out," I said, shaking a finger at him.

A woman stood on stage that I didn't know all that well. I think her game name was Mishre, and my recollection was that she'd opted out of the rank system after a nasty spat, declaring her own independent house. As a neutral party, she did make a pretty good choice for officiant.

Annabelle, Ernie, and I were joined on stage by his witness, Count Merlot. Merlot, a plump cheerful man, had been his lieutenant since long before Ernie had seized control over the Indy vampire group. He wasn't a guy to mess with. Not to mention, his +1 sticker. Then again, if everyone had one, it stopped being an advantage. Maybe that's why it was given out so easy, I thought.

Mishre greeted the crowd as the rest of us formed a row behind her, Ernie and I flanked by our witnesses. She had a high, musical voice, and it was a pleasure to listen to her speak. It almost calmed the butterflies that had sprung up in my stomach. The fluttering was enough to make me worry I'd caught something from Stein. *But the flu takes days to incubate, right?*

Mishre turned to face us now, smiling. I could tell she enjoyed getting to be in the spotlight. Her curly strawberry blonde hair gleamed in the stage lights like a halo.

She talked in a low voice to us before continuing. "Your Grace, I'm told there have been a number of people taking sick, so we should make this a short ceremony."

Ernie's face remained neutral as he said, "Very well, proceed."

What's going on?

Mishre proclaimed, "Tonight, we are here to witness the joining of two immortal undead in an unholy union, let us rejoice!"

There was some chuckling among the crowd.

"If there are any here who know why they may not be wed, please speak now!"

I waited, wondering if Stuart would reconsider, but the sound of the fountain roaring was all that answered the officiant's question.

"Splendid!" she cried. "Duke Ernest, do you take the Baroness Sofia to be your wife, for good or ill, blood or famine, as long as you both remain undead?"

The Night Duke cracked a smile at this vow and looked at me, his clammy hand folded over mine. "I do indeed," he said. Despite the lightness of the ceremony, and despite the points he'd scored, Ernie somehow still made it sound creepy. I shivered.

Maybe it's just skillful role-playing.

Mishre turned to me. "And do you, Baroness Sofia, take the Night Duke as your husband, your blood as to his blood, assuming the rights and duties of Duchess of the Indianapolis Court of vampires?"

The butterflies had grown fangs, and my stomach cramped with anxiety and nausea. I shouldn't be so nervous for a fake wedding. I'd 'married' Stuart in-game, despite just living together in real life. Maybe it was being up on stage, or maybe it was worrying about what Queenie had planned?

There were some coughs out in the audience. Even a few groans. Annabelle nudged me.

Oh. Yeah, my turn.

"Yes. I mean, *I do!*"

From the other side of Ernie, Merlot let out a low moan. I glanced over, and saw him clutch his stomach.

Out in the crowd, I noticed a rising glow. Queenie had begun to shine with her own unearthly inner light, just as she had in my dream. Her grin was wicked and triumphant.

Mishre's voice shook and she put a hand on her own stomach. Her +1 sticker fluttered off her gown as she struggled to remain standing through the finish. "Then by the powers granted me by this Court, I pronounce you Duke and Duchess of Indianapolis. You may now kiss your bride!"

I turned to see my new husband, his complexion paler even than usual. For some reason, when he kissed me, I let him do it, rather than stage-kissing him. It was just a peck, Ernie didn't take creepy advantage of the moment.

Merlot fell to the stage with a thud. Mishre made a hasty exit down one side stair, and excused herself with a hasty murmur.

I turned to look at Annabelle. She looked alarmed and had her left hand tucked between the buttons of her tuxedo coat, touching her belly. "Skye," she whispered, "What's going on?"

I looked out into the crowd, and saw at least half of my vampire friends sat or lay on the ground, and many of the rest held their stomachs. I heard the sounds of someone vomiting not far away.

Queenie shone like an evil star that had come to rest on the ground, her cold light illuminating her many slaves, who had all turned to wolves during the ceremony.

Queen Howl crowed with glee, "You all have a choice, having drank Socrates' demise! Join me, or die!"

Chapter Fourteen

The Night Duke clutched his stomach and fell on his ass on the stage next to me, then fell over on his side, curled into the fetal position and groaned.

It sunk in that we'd all been poisoned by Queenie, using the spicy 'blood' punch. Rather than hunt each victim down, she'd opted to take over as one big coup, making her offer to everyone at once.

Damn. Think fast, Skye!

Annabelle slumped into me. She put my hand on the hilt of the fireplace poker. "No way am I giving up to her, I'm not gonna be a slave like Stuart and the others. I'd rather die."

I kissed her as though that could change things. "No!"

She smiled and leaned harder into me. "Go get her, my hero," she said.

"No, you're the hero, you're a firefighter. You run into burning buildings. I'm just an unemployed barista."

She punched me. "Remember the fairy tale? I was wrong. Everything else may be bullshit, but you're still a hero. Believe in yourself, Skye, I do."

She slumped to the stage, holding her stomach and moaning. *I have to save her!* I took the fireplace poker from her and leaped from the stage toward Queenie, sweeping it in wild swings.

My vision blurred a bit, and the night became deeper, the stars brighter, and all I saw of people were auras. Then, those auras took on a solid single-color form, like holograms. Or ghosts.

The glowing spirits stood over their bodies, looking confused.

Her wolves formed a snarling line, and one lunged at me, teeth bared, claws extended. I slashed with my iron weapon, and the smell of burned meat and hair filled my nostrils as the metal branded the creature. It let out a pitiful yelp, and then fell to the ground, writhing in front of me.

"Next!" I cried, advancing.

The wolves backed up, but surrounded me, growling and snapping their teeth. I kept walking forward, menacing them with the poker. I couldn't watch them all at once, though. I felt hot pain shoot up my leg as jaws clamped onto my calf and teeth sank into my skin and muscles, scraping bone.

I swatted behind me and felt the poker connect with a solid thud and crack. The jaws let go, and another smoldering wolf body lay behind me. The others backed off a bit more, still growling with menace.

I kept on toward the icy light of Queenie. I rushed the line ahead of me and struck two more down. They fell with heart-wrenching cries, and I decided I hated this. These wretches were people who'd been given an impossible choice. It wasn't a good choice, but who could blame them for choosing not to die?

More wolves joined the circle, perhaps turned from those who didn't want to die from poison. Soon, maybe there'd be hundreds of wolves around me. Soon enough, I'd be overwhelmed, and I could imagine those sharp teeth being used to tear out my throat.

Well, I'd made my choice at last, given Queenie her answer. I'd go down fighting, like the MacLeods of old.

Hold fast. That's what my clan's motto was, I remembered now. I hoped Bask's story was true, because to do that, I'd have to risk it all on my hunch.

"My people!" I cried out. "I am your new Duchess! To me! To me! We are fierce vampires, we can not let these wolves defeat us. Do not serve this usurper, but help me defeat her! We shall hold fast and win the night!"

A ripple in the air passed through me like a shockwave. Eerie shouts and cries reached my ears as my vampires began to fight. I heard screams and strangled cries, howls and yelps. They might have teeth and claws, but we had numbers, and nothing to lose but our already forfeit lives.

The wolves around me soon fell back to surround Queenie, facing out, rather than holding me in. I felt pride swell within me as I saw ghostly vampires swarm in on them. Many were thrown back or shaken like rag dolls in the vicious jaws of the wolves, but more came on to take their places.

I menaced the wolves in front of Queenie with my poker. "Stand aside!" I cried, as an electric thrill filled my body. I hoped my warrior woman namesake would be proud of me, though I didn't have the training as a fighter or a general. I'd rallied my friends, and it looked like we might just win.

Queenie cried out, "Fools! This is not a game! We are not throwing chops! You *will* die if you do not choose to serve me!"

My army hesitated, and the wolves used that opportunity to counter-attack, widening their circle around Queenie and Stuart, and I had to fall back as several wolves rushed me at once.

Queenie moved, and her defenders moved with her, a living, snarling, biting wall that mowed down the spirits of my vampires. She'd demoralized them, making them think about what was going on, while her army pressed the attack.

Some vampires must have had a change of heart, as their numbers continued to grow, despite earlier losses. I struck wolf after wolf, my iron poker filling the air with the stench of fallen wolves, but I couldn't keep this up forever. They just kept coming at me, and my arm was tiring.

"Help your Duchess!" It was Annabelle! I couldn't see her, but her voice came over the crowd clear and strong. "Does this look real to any of you dumbasses? She's our only hope, so fight for her!"

"Hold fast!" I cried again, and my vampire friends and I rushed the gang of wolves threatening me, forcing them back.

All of a sudden, I found myself in the eye of the storm. A clear field opened before me as I knocked down a wolf. The only ones in the clearing were Queenie, Stuart and myself.

Queen Howl narrowed her eyes and walked right up to me and grabbed onto the iron poker. Her hand sizzled as if it was straight from the fire, and I felt more nausea come over me as I smelled her flesh burning. Her grip was unbreakable, and she ripped my weapon from me and hurled it with terrible strength over the crowd. I heard a clang and a splash as it went into the canal.

Queenie faced me, just a foot from me. The light from her was blinding, and her face showed sharp wolf teeth, and her horns became more solid and real. Her fingers were claws, and she swiped at me.

I jumped back and panic caught fire within me. *What can I do now?* I heard a rustling and Minnie peeked out of my silly little purse. She waved something in her hands. Little paper packets.

Salt!

I took the packets from her and tore them in half and let the salt fall to the ground. Queen Howl stopped, startled.

"Count it up, bitch." I said.

There was fear in her eyes. She fought to hold eye contact with me, but her gaze dropped to scan the ground. Her body twitched and convulsed. She bent and I saw her lips move. *Holy crap, Annabelle was right!*

Then, with a grimace, she closed her eyes and took a deep breath. She stood up. "The best part of being Queen," she said, "is delegating. Stuart, be a dear and count those for me."

Stuart gasped at the command and fell to his hands and knees, bewildered at the galaxy of almost invisible salt grains. Queen Howl threw back her head and screeched, and I knew it was over.

Then something flew over the top of the circling wolves. I caught it out of instinct. I held a swing-top bottle of Heath's gruit. I opened it, started to drink, then stopped.

I had to take the gamble.

I threw the bottle onto the salt pile, and it broke, spilling out its contents among the shards of glass.

"None!" declared Stuart as the salt all dissolved into the puddle of beer. He caught my eye and nodded. I nodded back. He drew the sceptre from its holster on his belt and flung it toward me.

Queenie's victory scream changed pitch to one of dismay as the rod tumbled end over end toward me. I grabbed it out of the air and a brilliant blue blade sprang from it.

I didn't hesitate now, but struck before Queenie could do anything. I swung the Fairy Hilt and its blade of crackling spirit energy right through Queenie's waist.

She stood there a moment, burbling and spitting hateful curses at me, but only for a second.

Then she fell in half.

I let out a whoop I didn't know I had in me, whirling the magical blade around in a circle above me. At the sound of my scream of victory, all around me, everything stopped. Wolves turned to peer at Stuart, me, and their fallen Queen.

Then she moved. I couldn't believe it, and as in a dream, I stood and stared, rooted to the spot. Unable to do anything but watch in horror, despite the warnings screaming in the back of my mind somewhere, I watched as Queenie's arms lifted her upper torso.

She spat at me, and then walked with her arms as legs, hands as feet, scuttling faster than I'd have thought possible.

Toward Stuart. His eyes popped open in fear and he scrambled backward, unable to get to his feet fast enough.

I came back to myself and hurled myself and the fairy sword at Queenie, but I missed and hit the ground hard where she'd been. I looked up to see that her upper half had leaped onto Stuart. Her claws gripped his head and he screamed. It was the worst sound I'd ever heard; I knew I'd never be able to drink enough to wash it out of my brain.

I scrambled toward them, hampered by my heels and the restricting satin of my dress, but I was too late. For an instant, I thought she was pulling him in for a kiss, but his head flipped back and she tore his throat out with her sharp teeth.

Blood gushed from the wound and Stuart gurgled his last breath, eyes wild and insane.

I found my footing in a crouch. I swung the hilt, the blade of energy passed through her neck and her head fell from her torso. The hideous light from within her skin faded out like a TV tube in the dark.

From the stump of her neck, I took back the chain holding the computer chip talisman and shoved it in my pocket.

"Mine," I whispered to the corpse. My whole body shook with a sob. "Mine, damn you."

Then, I knocked her head and body off of Stuart. Her body fell apart, there on the pavement by the canal. No, it was more like she *dissolved,* her flesh boiled and consumed itself in the night air.

Stuart's eyes stared, open and glassy, his flesh torn and bloody.

I wept over his body and didn't care about the sounds around me. I was aware of movement and murmuring.

I felt Minnie climb up my arm and onto my shoulder. She petted my hair and whispered in my ear, "I'm sorry too. But you have to see what's going on, sis."

Then a great cheer rose up that I couldn't ignore. As I looked up, I thought everyone must have gone crazy. There were a couple of dozen people dancing around me, wearing torn, bloody clothing. It looked like we'd decided to become a zombie club, instead of vampires. Bodies lay all around them, some also bloody. Not all of them were motionless, some stirred and moaned.

Those cavorting around me cheered and shouted their thanks to me.

"They're cheering for you, big dummy, you freed the wolves from Queenie's bargain!" Minnie was right. I saw the auras of the former wolves, and they'd joined the overall purple aura of the others.

Oh! The others still have auras! They're not dead!

I sat up, not daring to look at Stuart's body again, not yet. "Hey! Stop celebrating, there's still time! They need your help!"

The standing gamers froze and raised their gaze, looking at something behind me. I turned to see a dark mass on the water eclipse the fountain, something big and silent.

I don't know what it looked like to everyone else. Maybe they retained some Sight after losing their wolf-ness. Or maybe they saw people, or perhaps the boxes just levitated in mid-air. What I saw was a troupe of half a dozen gargoyles, climbing out of a flat-bottomed boat, each carrying a box. They opened the boxes and began unloading many bottles, which they lined up on the pavement.

Then a little man climbed over the side and ambled over to me. He tsked at the smoldering piles of ashes around me, all that was left of Queenie. He helped me up.

"Can...can you do anything for Stuart?" I stammered out, struggling to hold in more tears.

"Nae, 'tis a pity, but his fate was set when she laid the geas upon him, he was destined to die if ye should get the Hilt. Speaking of which, d'ye mind putting that away?"

I looked at the blade. I didn't know how to turn it off. I couldn't find a switch. So I just put it on the ground next to me, and when I let go, its brilliant blue light went out, and it was just a hilt once more.

"I'm sorry, lass. But ye did brilliantly! Look around ye!"

I saw most of my friends laying in pain or unconscious around me. Annabelle still lay up on the stage, scratches all along her arms and marring her beautiful face.

I excused myself from the King and took up two of the bottles and picked my way through the prone forms of vampires on the ground around me and up the stage steps to get to my girlfriend's side.

Her breathing shallow, her face contorted in pain, my Annabelle curled into a ball around herself. I stroked her cheek and she relaxed just a little. I pulled the cork on one small glass bottle and held it to her mouth. Her lips parted to allow me to pour the liquid into her. I saw her throat move as she swallowed. Relief spread across her features, and she uncurled, lying limp. Her chest rose and fell with stronger breaths, and a smile came to her lips.

I uncorked the other bottle and drank from it. For all the world, it tasted like Milk of Magnesia. The cramping in my stomach subsided, and the aches I didn't realize I had eased as my muscles relaxed.

"We won?" she asked, without opening her eyes.

I nodded, then realized she couldn't see that, so I said, "We did. Queenie's dead." I left out the part about Stuart, for now. "Bask brought antidotes."

I didn't have to tell the former wolves what to do, they followed my lead and brought bottles to fallen vampire gamers. I heard the pop of corks near me, and the relieved sighs as the potions began to work on them.

Bask had followed me, and he crouched down across from me on the other side of Annabelle. "I could nae have been prouder, lass. 'Hold fast' ye did, and so did many of yer friends, thanks to you. A mightier bit o' courage hasn't been seen since the days of your tales."

"I was wrong," said Annabelle, opening her eyes. "Skye really was the Chosen One, wasn't she?"

I felt a hot flush coming to my cheeks. "So why didn't you tell me about this prophesy sooner, King Bask?"

He let out a belly laugh. "Because I hadn't made it up yet!"

I stared at Bask, who now reminded me of nothing so much as an overgrown garden gnome as he slapped a knee and guffawed, gasping for breath as he laughed.

"What? You're shitting me!"

"Nae...nae, lass," he stammered out with an effort between gales of laughter. "Y'see t'was only a tale, but ye lived up to it!"

"Holy crap!" cried Annabelle, propping herself up on one elbow. She laughed too.

I felt ice in my hands and feet. "So..." I searched for words. "You're telling me I risked my life and the lives of everyone here, hundreds of people, on a lie?"

His laughter slowed and stopped, but crinkles of amusement showed at the corners of his tear-filled eyes. He wiped at them. "Nae, nae, not a lie. T'was just a story that hadn't come true yet. Ye humans need things to believe in. Stories ye know to be false still raise yer spirits. Sometimes it takes a story to get ye to believe what you should already know. You needed to know you could do it. I knew ye could, I believed in ye, lass. After all, we are kin of a sort."

I stared at him, sure that I looked as stupid as I felt. I said "Huh?" and heard Annabelle say the same thing in unison.

He snickered and giggled. "I said as much on the gondola, lass. Yer great-great-great, and so on, grandmother of the same name as ye, she was me father's father's lady love. Sad that ye lot live so short a span, he died of a broken heart long before yer family came to this side of the world."

Annabelle giggled now. "See? It all makes sense now. You're a *fairy*, Skye!" She winked at me and puckered her lips in a kiss.

I didn't know what to say to that. My face still felt hot. Bask filled the gap by continuing, "Nae, not all fairy, just a teeny part, smaller than the wee girl on her shoulder." He winked at Minnie, and I felt her scurry behind my head, hiding in my hair. She's not used to being noticed.

Annabelle looked at my shoulder and squinted, then shook her head. "So, I guess we'd better thank you for the antidote, King Bask. Lucky you knew what to bring...," she said, watching him with narrowed eyes.

King Bask smiled. "It was ever part of the game that the winner take all. The stakes were high in our chess game. Either Queenie won and some lay dead and the rest joined her army, or I could save all o' ye. Well, almost all o' ye, sad ta say. He gave much to save ye, lasses."

We repeated our earlier "Huh" with equal brilliance.

His smile was sad. "Aye. His bargain that ye should have the chance to escape her castle alive was bought with a tie to the Hilt. From that moment on, his fate was sealed."

"Stuart did that for me?" I felt a lump of ice growing in my stomach.

Bask nodded. "Aye."

"How the hell do you know all this?" Annabelle asked.

King Bask spread his hands in front of him. "Pillow talk is a terrible thing."

We just sat there looking at him a long while. I made the connection at last. "King Bask and Queen Howl...she was your *wife?*"

The little King almost looked embarrassed. "Aye. Love is a strange attractor. I could nae resist her, nor could she resist me, though that was all we agreed on."

"So...should I be sorry, or should I be pissed at you for being part of this...game?" I said, the ice burning within me. I looked back to where Stuart lay, the Hilt on the ground next to him. Its gems shone even in the moonlight.

"Ye can feel how ye like. I don't know how to explain the workin's of my world to you, Skye. Just know I was ever in your corner, and though I loved her, I knew it had to end this way. Or much worse."

I felt a tangle of emotions writhing inside me. But more than that, I felt bone tired. Too tired to unravel that knot at the moment.

I looked around me now and saw that a lot of my fallen friends were sitting up and talking and examining their scratches from the battle in shadow, healed in the real world. Some of Queenie's former slaves still tipped bottles into the mouths of other unconscious gamers.

Blue and red lights flashed up above us, over the edge of the wall around the canal fountain's circle. Flashlights swept around as police descended stairs on either side.

"Now I must be takin' my leave, lass. Should ye ever need anything, just take the number 28 to Holliday Park. Ye'll find me or word'll get to me."

"Wait! What'll we tell the police?"

He smiled. "Another tale. What most here will remember anyway. Someone spiked the punch with 'shrooms and while everyone freaked out, a pack o' wild dogs attacked, killing poor Stuart."

Oh Stuart.

She must have seen the tears well up in my eyes, because I found my arms full of Annabelle, who held me in a fierce hug.

And with a wave, the Transit King slipped off into the darkness.

I didn't let myself fall apart again, though the temptation was strong. I did let her hold me a long while before I spoke, murmuring in her ear. "I guess he's right, it could have been a lot worse."

She pulled her face back and looked in my eyes for a long serious moment. Then she kissed me. I melted into her, and for a blissful moment, the world faded around us.

After we came up for air, she said, "You were great, Skye. A regular superhero, kicking ass in heels and hot red lipstick!"

I laughed. "Sure, we won. Guess all I need now is a job and a place to live."

She stuck her tongue out at me. "Skye. You think I'm going to let you live on the street? Plenty of room at my place."

I looked into her hazel eyes and wanted to just get lost in there. "Thank you, honey. You don't have to...."

"No, I don't have to. Whether or not we work out, you're a friend, and I'll take care of you. I owe you my life, after all."

"No, you don't! You saved me, right? And without me, you'd never have gotten tangled up in all this."

She grinned. "I hope the game isn't always this rough. I had no idea you nerds partied so hard. Next time, I wanna play a vampire."

A grin to mirror hers spread across my face. "Next time?"

"Sure, why not? Aside from the poisoning, it was a hell of a time."

We laughed together. A voice interrupted us. "Um, ma'am. Your Grace."

I looked up, not letting go of Annabelle. Wolfie-boy Deke crouched near us. He said, "I just want to thank you, on behalf of the rest of us...we never wanted to do any of that. She made us fight against the vampires. If we didn't, we'd have to die too."

"You assholes made your choice," said Annabelle, separating herself from me to stand up. She offered me a hand, and I let her pull me up.

"I won't tell you it's okay," I said, drawing out my words as I sorted out how I felt. "You'll have to figure that out for yourselves. She had me where she wanted me, and I didn't end up having to make that choice until I found myself in a position to actually fight back. But I didn't choose the same, Deke. I thank you for the help you've given me, but you're free now, and we're even."

He nodded.

"Is that all you interrupted us for?" asked Annabelle.

He shook his head. "No, I was wondering, if you need another vampire or something, in the game? I could work for you, maybe?"

I winked at Annabelle and slipped an arm around her waist before answering him. "Bite me!"

About the Author

E. Chris Garrison writes fantasy and science fiction novels and short stories.

Her urban fantasies feature ghosts, demonic possession, and sinister fairy folk delivered with a "lightly dark" side of humor.

Her latest series is Trans-Continental, a steampunk adventure with a transgender woman protagonist. The series is set in one of the worlds featured in Chris's dimension-hopping science fiction adventure, Reality Check, also published by Silly Hat Books. Her Reality Check reached #1 in Science Fiction on Amazon.com in 2013. Silly Hat Books released Alien Beer and Other Stories, a collection of her short stories, in 2017.

Blue Spirit is followed by Restless Spirit, and Mean Spirit, to form The Tipsy Fairy Tales Trilogy.

Chrissy lives in Indianapolis, Indiana, with her wife, step- daughter and many cats. She also enjoys gaming, home brewing beer, and finding innovative uses for duct tape. Keep up on the latest news and releases from Chris at https://sillyhatbooks.com/

Photo Credit: (c) Ellie Sophia Photography
www.elliesophia.com

This book is part of an author-cooperative urban fantasy universe. Characters created by E. Chris Garrison (including Skye MacLeod and the Transit King) and R.J. Sullivan (including "Blue" Shaefer and Rebecca Burton) interact in a shared world. For example, Chris's Transit King appears in R.J.'s Haunting Obsession, while R.J.'s Rebecca Burton lends a hand in Chris's Mean Spirit. So if you love what you just read and want the entire story, here's a handy guide and timeline to:

The Skye-Blue-niverse

Haunting Blue by R.J. Sullivan *
Four 'Til Late by E. Chris Garrison**
Haunting Obsession by R.J. Sullivan
Sinking Down by E. Chris Garrison**
Blue Spirit by E. Chris Garrison
Me and the Devil by E. Chris Garrison**
Virtual Blue by R.J. Sullivan*
Restless Spirit by E. Chris Garrison
Mean Spirit by E. Chris Garrison

*Also part of The Collected Adventures of Blue Shaefer by R.J. Sullivan
**Part of the Road Ghosts Omnibus by E. Chris Garrison

Enter the Skye-Blue-niverse at:

**https://sillyhatbooks.com/
and
https://rjsullivanfiction.com/**